After the Ball

AFTER
THE BALL

Eileen Dewhurst

A Lythway Book

CHIVERS PRESS
BATH

C.1

First published 1976
by
Macmillan London Limited
This Large Print edition published by
Chivers Press
by arrangement with
the author
1989

ISBN 0 7451 1007 X

British Library Cataloguing in Publication Data available

— CHAPTER 1 ——————————

'The same again, Stephen?'

'No, on me. Two draught bitters, please.'

'I'm sorry, sir. I'm just closing.'

The newly-formed Frensham repertory theatre club had come to the end of its first meeting—an informal get together of players and played-to after the last performance of the run. The actors had withdrawn first, despite the informality, as if to preserve some vestige of their mystery, and now the members were beginning to drift out of the foyer. The two cheerful male voices seemed to get louder against the declining hum of conversation.

'Culture in the provinces, you see, my dear Stephen.'

The bar screen rattled down.

'I never doubted it. And there were some really quite interesting things.'

'Interesting people?'

'Not noticeably, but who was that big tall girl with the good features who hardly spoke a word to anyone and then suddenly went on and on about Tolstoy?'

'Oh, that was Angela Canford.'

'You know her?'

'Lifelong acquaintanceship.'

'Tell me about her.'

'Why?'

'No reason.'

'There isn't much. Has intellectual aspirations—as you'll have gathered—hopes to go to Oxford and read Russian. Too clever for me. A bit immature, though—boarding school type.'

'Jolly hockey sticks? She didn't strike me . . .'

'Oh, not *that* type. Just that girls who have been tucked away in boarding schools tend to be—well, they tend to be difficult. And no style.'

'I don't know.'

'D'you want to meet her?'

'Oh, next time down, perhaps, I'm not bothered. Anyway, I've got to be on my way in the morning.'

'One other thing, Stephen—she *is* old man Canford's daughter.'

'Of the Canford millions?'

'None other. Still sure you'll wait till next time?'

'Yes, thanks.'

The voices faded as the men moved away. A light snapped off overhead. On the far side of the fretworked partition Angela crept trembling out of the shadows and into the ladies' cloakroom. Eavesdropping, even if involuntary, was a horrible experience.

Under the dim light her image swam in the spotmarked glass, and it was several minutes before she was able to examine her serious face.

Good features.

Straight nose, yes, eyes set well apart, chin line firm. But the unaccustomed colour in her face had ebbed and she had two pimples.

No style.

Hair limp and mousy. Clothes—covering her.

Intellectual aspirations.

Yes, she did make a bit of a thing about reading Russian. She was uncomfortable, realising it. And occasionally she did feel superior to other people. But at the same time she felt awkward, wary, expecting her contemporaries to be more sophisticated than she was . . .

Odious Simon and his odious friend Stephen! *I'm not bothered.* Well, she had snubbed Simon at a party only the other day, dodging out of the slightly tipsy embrace he had attempted because she was the nearest female. So perhaps in the circumstances he had been lenient.

The Canford millions.

Angela banged out of the ladies' room and marched through the empty foyer to the doors. The commissionaire had closed all but one.

'Goodnight, miss, you're the last!'

It was raining, a mean drizzle, and the swish of the windscreen wipers went with the familiar phrase in her head.

'Your father is very, very rich.'

That was the form it always took, because that was the phrase in which she had first learned of her difference from her friends.

She hadn't learned it from her parents. She had come into the formroom at school one day when she was fourteen and found everyone clustered together at the far end, and she had known, from the challenge vibrating in the air, that they were like this because of her. She had faced them across the gap and one girl, the spokeswoman, had detached herself from the group and come up to Angela and said—half, it seemed, as statement of fact, half as accusation:

'Your father is very, very rich.'

4

Angela hadn't been able to see how this could possibly warrant a group on one side of the room, and herself on the other.

'Well, so is yours. If you think of the condition of most people. So is Jane's, and Sheila's—all our fathers are rich.'

'Not as rich as yours.'

She was leaving the village behind now, and the road narrowed and darkened. The cold perspiration of her eavesdropping had dried on her body, and she shivered.

Her father had inherited money, and had increased it. He used it to promote the public good, quietly. He told Angela so when she transmitted the challenge to him as soon as possible after the encounter in the formroom. He had been very angry.

Turning into the lane, Angela remembered herself earnestly telling him not to worry, half wishing she had kept her newly acquired knowledge to herself. She had always wanted to give her father pleasure rather than pain. Her mother as well. They were two of her few friends, and so far there had been no confrontations on the scope of their authority. Angela had never tested it; in fact her parents, in the couple of weeks since her return from school, had been urging her to get into the local

5

circle of young people, to join in this and that . . .

A bit immature—boarding school type.

Angela drove into the garage rather too fast, and slammed on the brakes. Was that what it was, that made her reluctant to go out and mix with her contemporaries? Or was it the arrogance of the *intellectual aspirant* (if only she didn't have such a good memory)? Perhaps it was both: certainly, at parties for instance, she could feel bored and scared at the same time.

Her parents were in the sitting-room.

'Did you have a good time, darling?'

'Not so bad.'

'How were the company without their scripts?' her father asked her.

'That part was interesting. The questioning was rather earnest.'

She re-enacted one or two scenes, then flopped into a chair, squirming in the sudden recall of the two confident men's voices.

'But I'm not being fair, I made a fool of myself. I started to talk about Tolstoy at one point, and I went on and on. He wasn't even a playwright.'

'Weren't you pleased to see all your old friends?' asked her mother.

'I don't know. I don't seem to fit in.'

'Nevertheless,' said her father, 'we belong to the village, and I wish us to play a part in village life. You must try, my love.'

So Angela engaged herself to provide Meals on Wheels once a week, and accepted invitations, and went to the Playhouse again at the end of the next run.

And after the performance Tim Folkard introduced her to a man called Gerald Massinger upon whom Tim, striking up a conversation during the interval, had prevailed to stay behind for the second meeting of the theatre club.

Gerald Massinger was better looking, more assured, better informed and more intelligent than any man Angela had yet encountered who could be said to be of her own generation—although he was older, well into his twenties. When the actors withdrew he and Angela spent a half-hour talking to each other, and he bought her a drink. It seemed to Angela that they talked about every impersonal thing under the sun. He didn't show by the tiniest variation in his cheerful, courteous expression that she interested him in any personal way, but they were still talking when people started to leave. By the time they reached the doors everyone had disappeared, and on the steps he kissed her lightly on the lips as he said good-night.

The world changed with the gesture, so unlike the clumsy efforts late on at parties or in cars, with their accompaniments of heavy breathing and fumbling hands. But then, she was never able to understand, let alone share, the claustrophobic mood of need and urgency, it frightened and repelled her. Gerald didn't need her. He touched her cheek with his finger, smiling slightly.

'I'll ring you sometime, my dear. In the book?'

'Yes. Yes.'

He saw her to the car, and she drove off in a turmoil. She must—she must—see him again. He was in neighbouring Dolchester, at least for another month, she had heard him tell Tim.

But one week turned into two, and he didn't ring. Angela went assiduously to parties and meetings in the hope that he might be there, but he never was. The Playhouse went into summer recess. Angela's new, painfully sweet preoccupation began to lose its edge. And then Mrs Ashton rang up to tell her that Mike couldn't partner her at the Bella Ball because he had developed measles.

8

The Bella Ball was an anachronism, a mother's dream. For some mothers, it was the one night of the year when they saw their daughters as they had once imagined they would frequently see them—gowned, cleaned, hair dressed and shining, eyes down. And if in embarrassment rather than shyness, the effect was the same.

The proceeds from the expensive tickets went to a consortium of local charities. Angela's father had for many years seen to it that little was lost en route in expenses. Consequently, the position of his family at the ball was an important one. Mrs Canford drew the raffle tickets and Angela when younger had handed a sheaf of flowers to the wife of the chairman of the council. This presentation had, however, in recent years been discontinued— Angela had grown into such a big girl, although this had not been stated in so many words in the proceedings of the ball committee.

Mike Ashton's father was a sort of second in command to Angela's, and Mike and Angela had made, for the third year running, the comfortable agreement to take care of each other's partnering problems. But this year Mike had measles.

As Angela heard the news a pulse began to beat in her throat. Automatically she offered condolences to Mrs Ashton, messages of cheer to be relayed to Mike, but her mind was busy with what she knew she was going to do.

Because she had Gerald's telephone number. Over coffee in the theatre Tim had asked Gerald where he could get in touch with him, and Gerald had taken Tim's packet of cigarettes and written a number on it and tossed it back. Angela had been between them and had helped the packet on its way. In doing so she had noted and memorised the number Gerald had scribbled on it. Not really because she thought of using it, more because it was there, in the way she read advertisements in trains and buses, and the squares of newspaper in outside lavatories.

She had wanted to use it, of course. She had traced its outline on the dial, longingly. But only now was there a situation in which she could just—just—make a move. The fact that Mike had measles was the deciding factor. Measles was not an excuse one would invent to cloak long-term lack of partner. It was so verifiable. It was clear that Angela had been left in the lurch at the latest moment.

It was no good trying until the evening. She struggled through the rest of the day, then went to the telephone. If there was no reply, or he refused her invitation, she might find herself even feeling relieved. But she had to try.

The bell was answered almost at once.

'Hello,' a voice said inquiringly. Angela had forgotten the particular pleasure of Gerald's voice.

Her own was husky.

'Gerald, this is Angela Canford.'

'Sorry?'

His politeness was cold in her chest.

'Angela Canford. We met at the Playhouse.'

'Oh, yes.' There was a pause that seemed lifelong. A few square inches of pattern on her mother's bedroom carpet passed into Angela's memory. 'I remember,' he said at last. His voice was without expression. 'How did you get my number, Angela Canford?'

'Very easily. I'll probably tell you.'

'Why did you get it?'

She found his directness a help.

'*Tout simplement.* My partner for the Bella Ball has developed the measles, and I'm ringing up to ask you to step in at the last moment and make up the party. Our party, of course.'

'Thank you, I'm flattered. But why me?'

This was more difficult, but she managed it with a canter. 'It's Frensham's

11

grandest social occasion, and I thought you would look better in a dinner jacket than any of the others.'

There was another slight pause.

'All right, Angela.' A slight tremor in Gerald's voice made her think he might be trying not to laugh. 'I'll come to the Bella Ball—if you'll tell me how you got my telephone number.'

She told him.

—— **CHAPTER 2** ————————

On the day of the ball Angela was so excited she paid several visits to the wood in a vague attempt to put her elation into perspective.

The wood was at the bottom of the garden. A real wood, the sun reaching through the trees only here and there in concentrated dazzling shafts. It straddled the boundary with another property and had no outside access. Angela had never learned to be afraid of the wood noises of cracking twigs and stealthy creaking undergrowth. For many childhood years she had been certain that rare wild animals inhabited it. Now she knew that there were at least badgers, because she had watched them. She was happier in the wood than anywhere else she had yet discovered. The thought of it blunted the edge of her displeasure at the final effect of herself, dressed for the ball, in a full-length mirror.

Gerald in his dinner jacket, faintly, masculinely scented, was so attractive there was almost something cruel in his charm, as if he was free of human weaknesses, exemplified to Angela a few moments earlier by the unexpected vigour of a spot, the waywardness of her hair, and a host of small imperfections. Also, the fact that his smile was merely polite, that despite his courtesy he was clearly immune to her Angelaness (she had no charms, she was gloomily certain, for him to be immune to) increased his desirability.

Over sherry in the sitting-room she could see he was impressing her parents. He admired the garden, enthusiastically but with reserve enough not to be fulsome. Angela made muffled reference to the existence of the wood but her mother said, eagerly:

'It's Angela's stress spot. Any trouble, and she walks it off in the wood, don't you, Angela?'

Gerald looked at her with a possible

13

interest but Angela had not wished him to hear about the wood in this way, as if it was the weakness of a child, like toffee or icing. She made no comment and after a few seconds he turned back to her parents, who had none of the diffidence of the young at asking questions, or indifference to facts. Between her father and her mother Angela learned that Gerald worked in London, where he had a flat, but that his parents were about to retire to a house near Frensham.

'This being commuter country,' said Gerald, 'I've installed myself in the new home as caretaker until they move.'

Angela noticed a tic at work in his upper jaw. His hair, dark and thick, was the sort of length that would give him unremarkable access among his contemporaries or his elders. Most of the young men, Angela thought, looked less good in their unaccustomed dinner jackets than in their usual daily *déshabillé*. Gerald looked merely different. She saw him as impressive with any group he cared to join, but never of it, belonging only to himself. Like her, but entirely from choice.

They left in two cars. Gerald had the radio on and they didn't talk. They were announced as a quartet. 'Mr and Mrs Charles Canford, Miss Angela Canford and

14

Mr Gerald Massinger.' They made up a table party of a dozen with two other family groups.

The young people never attempted, at the Bella Ball, to get together. It would have been too unnervingly like yet unlike their usual assemblies, and anyway it was the older people's night and it was easier, as well as more amusing, to hang around them and dance with them, because it was their kind of dancing. Contact with contemporaries was by signs, and muttered remarks *en passant*, and in the cloakrooms.

Angela's first visit to the ladies' cloakroom came at the end of dinner. She coincided with a group of acquaintances who had formed an animated gaggle as they preened by the row of mirrors. This was not the sort of company in which Angela ever shone, or attempted to, but tonight she was an instant centre of them because of Gerald.

'Well, now!'

'Dishy!'

'Angela, where have you been hiding *that*?'

'Oh, you know Mike's got the measles . . .'

'So you went abracadabra and produced . . .'

Their smiling bold faces seemed without exception pretty, smooth, skilfully painted, their bodies small and slight. Angela looked doubtfully at her own tall strong body and wary eyes, in a surround of hair that was already untidy.

'He's a friend of my mother's,' she said, in case she was unable to produce Gerald again.

When she got back to the table Gerald asked her to dance. He held her close to him because he was a good dancer and they didn't talk because of the crush of people and the volume of the music, but Angela had never known a man well enough not to consider herself inadequate when silent, and it took a dance with her father, rich in private allusion, to restore her spirits. Throughout the cabaret Gerald sat with his arm flung across her shoulders but he didn't look at her and Angela made herself accept the gesture as formal.

As the singer bowed out Mike Ashton's younger brother Jimmy arrived to ask Angela to dance. It was a gesture, no doubt parentally inspired, from the stricken Mike. Angela moved off with Jimmy, conscious of the unattractive duo they must present: she was taller than he was, and he was totally unable to dance, so that they walked round the floor treading on each other's feet and, as he held her rigidly at arms' length, she had too good a view of the crop of festering pimples on his chin. The bumps of the pimples, and the young beard struggling among them, blurred his profile, detracted from his kindly smile. The Ashtons were a nice family. Jimmy talked to her conscientiously about his school work and Mike's progress against his disease before they lapsed into a dogged silence.

The crowd was so thick it was difficult to see who was dancing with whom, and how intensely but, as if set for her view in a temporary clearing, Angela saw Gerald dancing with Christine Bolam, dancing with both arms around her waist, and Christine with both arms dangling down his back, and their cheeks together except when they drew apart and came together again to exchange little soft kisses.

Rage, pain, and a physical shudder passed through Angela.

'What's up?' asked Jimmy in concern.

'A goose over my grave, that's what they say.'

Angela smiled unseeingly at Jimmy Ashton and followed in his unrhythmic footsteps until the music at last came to an end. Gerald returned to the table at the same time as she did, drinks were replenished, conversation resumed, but for Angela the evening was over, its last hours a horrible endurance. She even wished that Gerald had not insisted on bringing her in his own car, she would prefer not to be alone with him again. Perhaps she could suggest that it would be easier if she went home with her parents. The only remaining satisfaction of the night was the gloomily masochistic one, when she was dancing with a friend of her father's, of seeing Gerald again with Christine Bolam, and then seeing neither of them. But he was back at the table just after she was, and she managed a little bright talk, avoiding her mother's warily concerned eye.

Angela and Gerald danced the last dance in silence, correctly, among couples who dropped wearily or amorously in each others' arms.

'I might as well go with the parents,' said Angela lightly, as the party straggled the streamer-strewn floor to the exit. 'Save you the bother of going out of your way.'

'No bother,' he said, but she determined to repeat the let out, as he had spoken mechanically while he looked over the departing throng.

Outside, shivering in the car park, Angela attempted to say goodbye, but

Gerald said: 'Don't be ridiculous', took her arm firmly, said a polite thank you to her parents, and led her across to his car. She felt beyond sensation.

'Do you remember the way?' she asked him, as they drove between the trees of the one-time country estate.

'I can always ask you,' said Gerald, 'if I get stuck. However, I thought we might look in at another party.'

She was not beyond sensation. But the wave of incredulous delight ebbed as quickly as it came. Christine Bolam!

'So who's giving a party on top of all this?'

'No one, so far as I know. This party's been going on all evening. Guy Hallam. Do you know him?'

'No. And I didn't think you knew anyone round here.'

'I don't.' He looked at her, and she thought it was only for the second time that evening. 'But I've met Guy once or twice and thought I'd like to look in at his party, if only because I don't know anyone round here. Are you game?'

'I'm game.'

He could have got rid of her first. The evening was miraculously rescued.

'Where does Guy live?'

'Not far away. Dolchester rather than Frensham. I think we can find it.'

The night was fine, but very dark. Angela snuggled into her seat. Through the windscreen she saw the sky, a high roof studded with diamond stars. They were still in the country, and Gerald drove fast along deserted roads. His intent profile was painfully attractive, and behind it were a million thoughts that she wanted to learn . . . She jumped as his hand pressed hers briefly. They were turning in at some gates.

'Are we here?'

'We're here.'

Gerald stopped the car, got out, and came round to Angela's side. As he let her out she saw he was carrying a torch. Indeed, the house was in total darkness.

'Are you sure the party's still going on?'

He murmured:

'One can never be sure of such things. But I was told they would be making a night of it. Let's have a look round the back.'

He took her arm, switched on the torch, and started to walk down the side of the house. The torch, a powerful one, illumined a sort of crazy paving under foot, bushes to one side, house wall to the other.

Their feet sounded loud in the absolute stillness.

Angela thought afterwards that fear gripped her while it was all still dark and silent, seconds before the curtain went up on the scene of violence that was to change her life.

Gerald said, suddenly and softly, 'What's that?', stopped, and switched off the torch. Angela heard first the eerie shriek of an owl and then, as that died away, a low, steady, sawing sound. Only it wasn't a sawing sound, it was someone trying to breathe, and all at once there were feet grating on the paving, and hoarse shouts, and the thud of blows. They stood silent, listening to the crescendo of struggle, and then Angela tried to run away, and Gerald tightened his grip on her arm, switched the torch on again, and shone it full ahead.

It seemed to Angela that it lit up a stage on which was playing the last act of murder, so remote was the man on the ground almost at her feet, his head towards her, his eyes unseeing, blood that the torch-light caught trickling out of his mouth on to the path. One of his legs was twisted under him and the man leaning over him had a knee in his stomach. Another man was lying nearby, flung on his back, blood flowing from his temple. As Angela stared in horror, waiting for the picture to dissolve as all nightmare pictures dissolved at their climax of terror, two other men began to drag him into the shadows beyond the arc of the torchlight. The other man so unbelievably near her, the one who was vomiting that dreadful glistening blood, cried out in hoarse entreaty, then fell back. The man above him rose panting, and suddenly Angela was no longer watching a ghastly tableau, she was gazing into hostile eyes, level with her own.

'Oh, no!'

The torch snapped off as she called out and they were running, pelting back in total velvet dark towards the gate and the car. Angela ran blindly, at Gerald's pace and under his momentum, and once swung out helplessly, grazing elbow and ankle against the pebbledash wall. There were shouts behind them from several voices but they were in the car, about to close the doors, as the pounding of feet began.

The gateway was wide and the drive short, but Angela admired the speed and certainty with which Gerald got them out on the road, without lights until he straightened up and started to move away.

'Well done!'

'So far. There was a car in the drive.' Gerald was looking every few minutes into the mirror. He accelerated. Angela felt a spasm of fear.

'So you think . . .'

'What do *you* think?'

'But they couldn't! We were . . .'

'What were we doing? Witnessing mass murder by the look of it. And where are we going now?'

'Home. Aren't we?' she faltered.

'If it can be done.'

'If . . . oh, Gerald!'

'I think we've got to assume that they're following us.'

'So what are we going to do?'

'We're not so far from your place.' His eyes were going from road to mirror to road. 'Your gates are on a bend, aren't they?'

'Yes. Yes.'

'So. I'll slow down to take the bend, and you get out. *Get out.*' He leaned across her and felt the door handle. 'Right?'

'Yes, all right, Gerald, but what about you?'

'I'll try and shake them off. If I can, I'll go home too. If not, I'll take them to the police station.'

The car protested at a sharp corner, rocked for a moment, righted itself. Gerald swore. Angela stretched out her hand towards the white knuckles on the wheel. She let it rest on them for a few seconds. There was no response, but there was no recoil.

'Gerald, thanks for thinking about me.'

'And I'm thinking about myself, my dear.'

'Perhaps they wouldn't recognise us. We were shining the torch on *them*.'

'Perhaps, but we've still got to get away from them.'

His profile was superb. Greek and white and firm, the current crisis conceded only by a small curl that had fallen on to his forehead. His eyes were going more and more rapidly from road to mirror to road. The car surged steadily ahead.

Angela stared into the long beam of light.

'Gerald . . . '

There was a bump, with a yielding finish, and Gerald swore again.

'That was a hedgehog!'

'So it was a hedgehog. For God's sake!'

He accelerated. Angela looked up at the starry sky, wiping the sudden reflex tears away with the palm of her hand.

24

'Gerald, if we give them the slip . . . They couldn't really have seen us . . .'

'They could. And they'll have seen the car number.'

'Maybe not. They're not in sight now.'

'They're not so far behind.' He shot her one of his rare, heart-stopping looks. 'Angela—I'd suggest, without sounding melodramatic I hope, it would be sensible not to say anything about this to your family—or to anybody else.'

'Oh. Why?' Angela's disappointment made her realise she had already started to look forward to sharing the nightmare with her mother and father.

'Well.' He looked at her again. 'Guy—the friend we went to see . . .'

'I'd forgotten about him!'

'Well you might have done!' His smile made her catch her breath. 'Guy gave me an idea he was in some sort of trouble—I think he was looking for a chance to talk to me. With hindsight, now, I think he was afraid of something.'

'Gerald . . . we didn't—see him—did we?'

'I don't think we saw him. But it was all so quick. Maybe the party would have been good cover for a heart-to-heart talk.'

'But there wasn't one.'

He smiled at her again. 'As you say. Which makes me wonder if we might have been even unluckier than we have been. As it is—I think the only people who should be told about this are the police.'

He accelerated again, concentrating on the road. A night insect thudded heavily against the windscreen and stayed there, spattering out in each direction. It was on Angela's side, impeding her vision, not Gerald's. Chance with them, for once. But it was chance that the insect, at all, had collided with the car. Chance that she had met Gerald at the Playhouse. Certain things you could never make provision against. Angela thought of Levin in *Anna Karenina*, attaining at the end a sort of radiant resignation that was a lifetime away from her, Angela, and perhaps not to be attained even in the end. She fought down her impulse to say something about *Anna* to Gerald. The occasion was hardly appropriate.

'So you'll keep quiet, won't you, my dear?' he was saying softly.

'What?' She had been miles away, incredibly, in the midst of her awareness of danger and pursuit. 'Oh, yes. I'm sure you're right.'

'Promise me?'

'I promise.'

'And make some suitable excuse to your parents for my not seeing you to the door.'

'That's all right. They'll have been in bed for hours.'

'Hardly. It's not much more than an hour since we left the ball.'

'It is!'

'No.'

They had been driving into the night for as long as she could remember. Metaphysical ideas surged in her head.

'Time goes as fast as the car just now, Gerald.'

He said, as if she hadn't spoken,

'Anything behind?'

Angela strained her eyes into the blackness behind them.

'Not that I can see.'

'I thought I saw them just now, but that was a very long straight stretch. It would mean they were still with us, but not near enough to interpret our every move.'

'You're coming to my corner.'

'I am. And when I do, and slow down, I want you to get out. Just get out, and run like hell into the gateway and hide inside the gates until the other car has gone past. And even then don't go walking up the drive. Can you dodge your way up among trees and things?'

'Yes. Oh, yes.'

He was beginning to slow down.

'Gerald . . . will you let me know. . . ?'

'I'll be in touch. Open the door *now*.'

She was in the ditch at the side of the road. By the time she had staggered to her feet with one heel through her hem, the car was out of sight and there was dark and silence. Hearing her dress rip further at each step, Angela hobbled between the gate posts of home and crouched down against the high stone wall.

Almost at once she heard the crescendoing roar of an engine, a brilliant beam spotlighted some form of beetle walking over the soil at her feet, then darkness and silence were restored.

Still feeling the rough protection of the wall through her shawl, Angela tried to get to her feet, but her shoe was now so implicated in her dress that she fell sideways into the rich earth to the accompaniment of more rending fabric.

She lay where she had fallen. Something crawled with a faint tickle up on to her leg, perhaps the beetle, but she didn't move. There was no further sound from the road.

What had happened? It was all so quick, so unlikely, that Angela could hardly believe that anything had happened at all, except that she was aware, for the first time, of throbbing pains where her elbow and ankle in flight had struck the house wall. The house where there had been no party, and no friend of Gerald's . . . But where there had been a man with angry eyes, killing another man . . . Gerald had told her not to speak to anyone about what she had seen. What had she seen?

And had she really escaped? And had Gerald? They had seen something, and they had been seen . . . But she would worry about this, and about his safety and hers—tomorrow.

Angela realised that she was making no effort to get up, despite the sensation of damp steadily penetrating her body, because she was so tired. She was so tired that all her worrying lay on the far side of sleep. Sleep . . .

With a supreme effort, concentrating her mind on the comfort of her bed, Angela struggled to her feet, released her dress, and began to totter towards the house, not without two further falls, keeping well away from the drive and among the denser trees, stinging her ankles on the nettles before emerging at the edge of the lawn. She crossed this at a limping sprint which brought her the invigoration of a giggle as she imagined how she must look, and arrived panting at the front door.

It was a bad moment, thinking she had forgotten her door key, but it was there in her bag when she made herself abandon her frenzied groping and feel each object in turn.

The house was blessedly silent and Angela reached her room without incident. She hung her ball dress, with its dirty trailing hem, at the back of her wardrobe, slinging her battered evening shoes underneath it. She cleaned her teeth, washed her face, and sank into bed.

Sleep came quickly and heavily, and it seemed only a moment later that her mother was drawing back her curtains. It was broad daylight, and there were breakfast sounds from below.

'Another Bella Ball over.' Her mother bent down to pick up Angela's evening bag from the floor. 'For the life of me, I can't remember one from another.'

CHAPTER 3

'You must have been late last night, darling.'

'Must I?' Her mother's implied reproaches were often couched in terms which lent themselves to short parody. But this time Angela decided to offer more. 'Well, we called in at a party on the way back. Some friend of Gerald's. It was all over, really, but we stayed for a drink.'

Was it necessary to be so circumstantial? The more lies you told, the more you had to remember. But there was more than an hour to account for, and Angela couldn't bear her mother to imagine that it had been spent with an affectionate Gerald—she was too fond of her mother to offer her an emotional deception on top of the necessary factual one. And Gerald's lack of continuing ardour—dear God, Gerald's disappearance?—would call forth a tactful concern from her mother which would be too unbearably misguided.

Her mother said, in surprise and probable relief:

'How nice, darling. I thought, earlier, that things weren't going so well.'

'No, Mummy, they weren't going "well". And they didn't go "well" later, either. Only Gerald wanted to call in at this party and it was between the Hall and home, so he took me. It was as simple as that.'

'But you enjoyed yourself?'

'I didn't not enjoy myself. I'm sorry if I had a down bit at the ball. But you know I get moods. Gerald's just a very sweet man.'

Angela felt the bright determination of her smile, almost as if she could see it. Her mother said, with a sigh:

'You're growing up.'

'I should hope so.'

Her mother was studying her face, and Angela was furious to feel a blush of guilty discomfort flooding upwards from her neck.

'You look tired, dear, dark under the eyes.'

'For heaven's sake, Mummy, one late night. You're always telling me to go out more, and then those nights you used to have, one after the other, such gaiety as never is today on land or sea!'

Her mother murmured:

'Don't jump down my throat, darling. I wasn't thinking so much of last night as wondering whether perhaps all your study hasn't taken a toll.'

'Oh, Mummy!'

Angela launched herself on her mother's open, slightly anxious face, and kissed it. Their relationship was emotional enough for her not to have to account for her swimming eyes. 'I *have* been bogged down with work but it's over for the time being and I needn't get going on Oxford entrance work for a month at least . . .'

'But you're working now.'

'Not really.'

She had to appear to be doing something other than worrying relentlessly about the consequences of the night before.

'You'll be better when you get to France.'

'Anne-Marie and I will have to work.'

Sunshine flooded the terrace. A small breeze riffled the tree-tops. A wren sang its thrilling, throbbing note. Angela shuddered.

'What's the matter, darling?'

'Goose on my grave.' And she had been upset by Gerald dancing with Christine Bolam!

'Will you go into town for me this afternoon?'

'What for?' The stab of fear was real. Men who killed men, violently, would stop at nothing.

'One or two things. More silks, for a start. We could go together.'

'No, dear, it's all right. I'll go for you.'

She didn't want to take her mother into danger.

Danger? Angela examined the word that had slipped into her mind, crawled there while her mother stitched a chair cover and Sarah rattled pots and pans in the kitchen and a starling on the lawn fed its demanding young.

What had Gerald managed to do after he had left her last night? Had he been followed home and dragged from his car? Or had he gone to the police station? If he had, how had he ever dared to come out again?

Angela got to her feet. On three sides the garden drowsed in summer sun and shadow. Behind was the house in its Virginia-creepered solidity. But no longer totally reassuring.

'What is it, dear?' Her mother's spectacles slid inquiringly down her nose.

'I'd better ring Mary about those books we want. She's going to London tomorrow and she said she'd see if she could get them.'

'Good.'

Her mother returned to her needlework and Angela looked at her in love and guilt. How easy it was, to tell lies!

The telephone shrilled away unanswered. There was no other action she could take than ring it at every unobserved moment of the day. Angela dragged back to the terrace and tried to read, glad of the interruption of lunch. But the moment came when her mother suggested it was time to go into town, if she was going.

'Oh, yes, I'm going.'

Having entered her mind, the word danger expanded inside it. Angela was almost surprised that the garage was empty of all but her car and the normal peripheral conglomeration of lawn mower and bags of fertiliser. How long had she been crouching inside the protection of the garden wall before the pursuing car went by? She didn't think it had slowed down for more than the taking of the bend, but she remembered the beam slanting over the plodding beetle. Had it slanted across her feet?

On the way into town she found herself looking constantly into the mirror at the cars behind her. She wished she had not been so addicted to detective fiction. She saw nothing to alarm her, but she was still a world away from yesterday, when she had looked in the mirror only to see if it was safe to stop or to turn.

Angela dived in and out of the few shops that had to be visited, and bolted for home. If—anything—was to happen, that was where she would prefer to be.

'What *is* the matter, darling?'

'Nothing, Mummy, honestly.'

If only she could tell! But she had given Gerald her word. She was glad to have no more commitments that day, and none the next or the next. She developed a private siege routine which involved sur-reptitiously making sure at bedtime that the front and back doors were locked, and the downstairs windows. She did it reluctantly, as admitting the possibility of danger, and by the third day she began, tentatively, to hope that she was being absurd. Gerald's telephone still bleeped unregarded, even throughout Saturday and Sunday, but he might have gone back to London, and he might not bother after all to tell her that all was well . . .

Surely, if all was well, Gerald would come back to Dolchester *some* time?

On the third evening her parents went out to dinner. Angela waited until she heard the car accelerate down the lane, then sped upstairs to the telephone.

But there was still no reply. If only she had his London number! If only she knew where he worked! But although she knew something of his taste in books and music, she didn't know what he did for a living . . .

Angela asked the operator to try the number, and the operator said there was no reply. Angela's reaction was getting nearer a feeling of disappointment for herself, and further from concern for Gerald's safety. She was a fool, to think he was in danger because he hadn't telephoned *her* . . .

The telephone bell shrilled, close beside her. Angela seized the receiver and it fell out of her trembling hand and clattered on to the table top. She picked it up again and spoke. A man's voice answered softly:

'Angela.'

'Gerald!'

'Gerald?' asked the voice in surprise, and a tongue of ice moved down the heat of her brief delight. 'No,' went on the voice, with the suspicion of a chuckle, 'this isn't Gerald, Angela. This is someone with your welfare very much at heart.'

The voice was caressing, well-educated like the voice of menace as portrayed by the cinema and TV to Angela's frequent delectation.

'Are you there, Angela?'

'Yes—yes.'

'Good. I have just one thing to say to you at this juncture. Don't—do anything. Don't—do—anything, Angela, that you wouldn't do in the normal way. Do you understand me?'

'Yes.'

'No unusual telephone calls. You tried to make one just now, didn't you? No out-of-the-way visits. And above all, Angela, no abnormal conversations with your parents. You don't want anything to happen to your parents, do you?'

'No! No!'

'That's good, then. You understand me, Angela. So remember.'

She said quickly:

'What's going to happen?' but the receiver clicked, then started to buzz. Eventually she put it back.

So. They had seen Gerald with her, seen or heard him slow down, seen him without her, and caught him. Perhaps— the sudden new thought, raising her to a yet higher pitch of nightmare, made her clutch the bedpost—after they had caught him they had made him talk to them (such people had methods), and that was how they had been able to telephone . . .

Angela ran out of the room and down the stairs, crashing through the garden door. From the kitchen Sarah called out:

'What's bitten *you?*' but Angela didn't wait to answer. She ran down the garden, more and more sick at each passing glimpse of what she had thought represented permanent order and safety, and under the gloom of the trees. She ran and ran, moaning, and the moans crescendoed to a scream, and the scream ended in a choke because the man who had stepped out from behind a tree clapped his hand over her mouth.

There was almost something of relief in it. Angela sagged backwards into the arms of another man who followed the first one out of the undergrowth. She shook her head behind the hand which was over her nose too and obstructing her breathing—it smelt of tree bark and tobacco—and it was removed. A voice said, low and intense:

'Don't—make any noise.'

'I shan't.'

Angela looked with interest at the man in front of her, still holding up his hand. Amazingly, her panic had subsided into a passive despair which at least freed her faculties to observe and her mind to comment.

The man's appearance gave her a small extra shock, he was so brutally handsome—repellently handsome because of the intense masculinity of it—brown skin, black wavy hair, glittering blue eyes. He made her think of a jungle animal—certainly he was a species as unfamiliar to her as a tiger, a species that she had never been so close to before. He was not a young animal, despite his lithe body—the skin sagged round his jaw and under his fierce blue eyes. Her mother would have called him unwholesome, and Angela was immediately aware that he had lived many years of a life she could only dimly imagine. He was sharply elegant in grey, and gold shone on his hands and wrists and among his teeth, which appeared in a satisfied grin as Angela continued to stand in acquiescent silence. But the hand caught her shoulder in a painful grip as she turned to look at the second man.

The second man was remarkable only for the total nullity of his appearance. Under-sized and pasty-faced, small-eyed with short flat grey-brown hair. Angela thought she could see him for the tenth time and not be sure that she had seen him before.

'Let's go,' said the first man.

'No!'

Angela shouted the word before she knew what she was doing, as the fear rose through the relief and took over, crowding her mind with images of pain and blood—her own, and indubitably to come.

'No!' she shouted again. And her mouth was forced open and her teeth so that for a moment she thought her jaw would break. And then she bit down on some fabric that was pulled hard against the tender corners of her mouth so that she felt sorry for horses, and perhaps passed out for a moment on that spasm of pity, because the next thing she knew was that she was being carried along under the trees, trying to tell them that there was no way out of the wood except up through the garden, that this arrangement had been made as carefully as the moon had been distanced from the earth, and that that was how it was. But she could only make grunts and moaning noises and she was carried on and on, under an unvarying pattern of sun and shade and tree-tops, until suddenly she was dropped to the ground and maybe there was another short gap because she was sitting up looking into the barrel of a gun and the man with fierce blue eyes was telling her to walk under her own steam to the car if she didn't want . . .

Angela nodded and formed a cross over her heart with her hand, and the other man undid the gag and she wondered if her mouth and jaw would ever stop throbbing and aching.

'Up!' said the first man, using the gun to illustrate his injunction, and Angela got up, but immediately fell back again against the grey raincoat, and they seemed to realise that this was something she couldn't help, because they waited while she leaned panting against it and until the attempts of the raincoated man to set her upright succeeded. Then they set off again, raincoat leading the way and Angela next, feeling the barrel of the gun between her shoulder blades.

And the wood came to an end, and there was a car on the verge of a lane, and Angela in the midst of her straightforward practical terror of these men and what they might do to her felt another, deeper terror that the wood had come to an end, almost as if the men were evil enough to have transcended a law of nature and per-

42

haps put in jeopardy all those vital assumptions which had made up, hitherto, the shape of her life. She stopped under the horror of such a thought, and was poked by the gun so that she fell forward and had to be hauled to her feet again.

The nondescript man opened the back door of the nondescript car, and the gun nudged Angela inside. The man with blue eyes got in beside her, and the last thing she saw was the little man opening the door by the driving seat, because the gag, this time, was drawn round her eyes, and fastened securely.

The car started up smoothly and silently and glided away, belying Angela's brief glimpse of it. As they rounded a sharp bend and in her blindness she put out a hand for balance, it was seized, and her other hand from her lap, and they were tied together, not painfully, with cord, and returned to her knees. But before they were relinquished they were held for a moment and the voice beside her said, not at all unkindly:

'Don't worry, doll. Just hang on. It'll be all right.'

The rough reassurance made her feel less utterly lost. The man's body was warm against her. The car was swaying less now, and Angela thought they were on a straight road, and that she could hear other vehicles whipping past. At one point there was a volley of honking and a curse, and the man beside her said:

'Take it easy, Joe.' He had a slight London accent.

The journey was long enough for the fear to creep back and fill her consciousness. What did a few words of comfort mean from a man like the man at her side? Some men would say anything, promise anything, to avoid seeing a woman weep. It could even have been a sadistic impulse, to lull her into a false sense of security . . .

When the car eventually drew to a standstill Angela was rigid with terror.

'OK, Joe.'

The pressure came off her side. It left her cold and she shivered. The seat springs groaned.

'For sweet Pete's sake, Joe, get to it. We don't want . . .'

The door beside Angela was opened from the outside and fresh air touched her forehead. She sat where she was, fearing her balance without eyes or hands, and was grabbed, not too roughly, by both arms and pulled out on to gritty ground. An arm each side of her, through hers, half carried her a very little way and bundled her through stiff doors which, to judge from a stifled yell and another curse from one of her attendants, had swung back before all ankles were clear.

Inside, where feet and voices echoed, they stopped and the bigger man's voice said:

'Take them off here.'

They had arrived somewhere. Angela's heart shot up into her throat, and beat there like the beating of wings. Her knees trembled, and even when her hands had been freed and the blind unfastened she could at first see nothing but a swaying maze of lights and shadows containing two looming and receding shapes.

The London voice said:

'Steady on, now, no need for that,' and as she went down two arms helped her land on her backside, on a low step, and they pressed her head down between her knees.

'I'm all right.' Vision came back to Angela a few inches short of a lolly wrapping and a blob of phlegm and she hastily raised her head. The two faces were looking down at her, the surrounds—the walls, the stairs spiralling up, the balustrade—were all of speckled plastic marble with a cold green frieze. The staircase was

45

narrow and uncarpeted, the ceiling a blur above five or six turns of the stairs.

The bigger man, whom Angela had started to call Gypsy in her mind because of the flashes of gold and his dark face and hair, said curtly:

'Get the lift!' and Joe looked round the corner and said:

'It's here.'

The lift was narrow and horribly claustrophobic. Gypsy pressed a button marked six, the top button, and they zoomed up, so that Angela felt the same surprise she had felt at the performance of the car.

They emerged on to a narrow, uncarpeted corridor, and Joe knocked at a plain door immediately opposite the lift. It had a spy hole at eye level and almost at once it was opened and an elderly man stood aside to let them in. He wore brown overalls and looked like a caretaker. Gypsy called him Sid. The hall was so tiny he was able to open a door opposite at the same time as he closed the front door behind them. Gypsy and Joe pushed Angela into the room and came and stood on either side of her.

The room was an office. Its occupant faced her over a large desk, to each side of which were filing cabinets and hard chairs, and an anglepoise lamp spilled a circle of light on to the papers between his hands. Behind him, the wide window was totally obscured by a venetian blind, pulled down to its maximum concealing capacity.

The man at the desk exuded a sort of settled prosperity, via his good suit and quiet tie and well-kept plump white hands and carefully groomed hair and slight but controlled over-weight of a comfortable middle age. He had a large rosy face and a kindly, inquiring expression. He was not unlike her Uncle John.

He smiled at Angela but she was unable to do anything but stare at him and his smile faded to a thoughtful gaze. Then, as if recollecting himself, he made a gesture and Joe moved forward quickly to bring one of the hard chairs to the front of the desk.

'Sit down,' said the man behind it, to Angela.

It was a low, full voice, entirely in keeping with the man's appearance, and Angela fancied it used a long Lancashire vowel. She sat down and the man said, confirming her impression:

'We're sorry we had to bring you here, Miss Canford, in so unceremonious a fashion.' He said 'unceremornious'.

Angela answered, with a blessed flare of anger which gave her strength:

'You're *sorry?*'

'Quick action was of the essence. There simply wasn't time to explain. You were in very grave danger, Miss Canford.'

'I *was?*' He had used the past tense. But Angela went on feeling ill-used, perhaps because there was a chance of making contact with this man, where Gypsy and Joe were ciphers. 'And now . . . ?' She was still terribly frightened.

'Well, we were in time.' He was such a comfortable person he could have been talking about keeping an appointment. 'And we will take care of you, now, until this disagreeable business is cleared up.' Angela went on staring at him and he said, leaning over the desk to her and intensifying the soothing qualities of his tone:

'You can relax now, my dear.'

'Relax! But—they tied me up!' Unfortunately there were no marks on the wrists she held out to him. 'They stuck a gag in my mouth! They—they abducted me! They made threatening telephone calls!'

'Ah!' Nodding his head, as if hugely satisfied, the man leaned back. 'You received threatening telephone calls, Miss Canford. One, I think, to be precise?'

'Yes, all right, one. One too many.'

He made her a little bow of assent.

'Miss Canford,' he said, 'we confess (he said 'con*fess*') to the abduction, to the—whatever methods were used to bring you here quickly and quietly'—he looked swiftly from Gypsy to Joe—'We do not confess to the telephone call.'

'Not . . . ?'

'No, Miss Canford.' The handsome, florid man leaned forward again, putting his fingertips together under his chin. 'We had better begin at the beginning,' he said, and sighed.

Angela said, in a rush:

'Just tell me . . . Gerald Massinger . . .'

'He is safe.'

She couldn't speak, but the man, watching her face, beamed his acknowledgement of her relief, and settled himself back again. He said, slowly, and as if selecting his words with care:

'Miss Canford, you and Mr Massinger unfortunately blundered into something very dangerous and—very big. Mr Massinger, after he had—er—dropped you at your home, drove his car to the central police station, parked outside, went in—and watched another car approach at high speed, slow down, appreciate the situation—and drive swiftly away. Mr Massinger told the police of what had happened. He gave them the address where he had witnessed these—er—incidents, and he told the police about you, Miss Canford.' He looked very seriously at her. 'The address which Mr Massinger gave the police as the place where these—events—had taken place was an address which the police had been interested in for some time, and where they had been expecting—developments—which could lead to the arrest of a group of very important and dangerous terrorists. But the time for this has not yet arrived, Miss Canford, the identities of all those it is hoped to apprehend are not yet known. You will appreciate—I cannot be more explicit. I can only tell you, without any ambiguity at all, that you and Mr Massinger were the witnesses of violent happenings among violent and desperate men, who are fighting with every evil weapon they can find and who still feel that they can win.

'When Mr Massinger had told the police all he knew, it was clear that he could not leave the police station in safety. It was also clear that you too might be in danger. The police started to keep a watch on you, Miss Canford, a discreet watch of course. Persons known to be involved in this—affair—were seen in the grounds of your house. A telephone call was intercepted which showed without any doubt that the woman in the car with Mr Massinger on that unfortunate night had been traced. You were in danger, Miss Canford, from men who would stop at nothing.'

The man behind the desk stopped at this point, and looked solemnly at Angela. So people did talk like that in real life! But . . . She said, quickly:

'But I *was* kidnapped. These men *did* seize hold of me—against my will . . .' She turned to Gypsy, whipping up her waning anger, and he looked at the ceiling, pursing his lips. 'I've been expecting—oh, all sorts of awful things to happen . . .' To her extreme annoyance, her voice choked on a sob.

'Awful things, Miss Canford?'

She said, feeling foolish even as she uttered the word, in the presence of this benign man:

'Torture!'

'Miss Canford.' The voice cooed like a disapproving dove. 'Torture? From Special Branch? We may have a reputation for toughness. It is as well if we do! But that doesn't run to . . .'

'Special Branch?'

Angela looked round again at the elaborately unconcerned Gypsy, at Joe with his little eyes fixed on the space above the big man's head, his utter lack, in every utilitarian line, of any kind of distinction. Of course!

'Miss Canford,' said the big man solemnly, 'we reached you in the nick of time.'

'You mean—if I'd perhaps run a different way through the wood?'

'Perhaps,' he said implacably.

'It's—it's *extraordinary*.' Angela felt winded by relief and understanding, but as much by the continuing fulfilment of the cliché situations of thrillerdom. The telephone call, the headlong flight arrested, the blindfold car journey, the revelation that the villains were the heroes—and, above all, Special Branch hiding away in a shabby, unlikely setting.

Was it only three days since life had been safe and ordinary? There was one more thing, though.

'I'd like—could I see Gerald Massinger?'

The big man—M, she was now calling him, irresistibly—looked at her for a moment without expression, then began to shake gently all over, and a low rumbling sound started deep down in his insides—he was laughing. Eventually the laugh broke surface, and he wiped his eyes. Angela waited, hoping it was a kindly laugh.

At last he said:

'Oh, Miss Canford, I don't think you quite trust us even yet.'

'Oh, I do!' Angela assured him, truthfully. 'Of course I do. It's just that . . . I've been so worried about Gerald. You see—he put himself in more danger to try and keep me out of it. He wasn't there when I phoned . . .'

'Of course, of course. We should have had him in here moments ago to reassure you.' M looked over at the small drab figure beside Angela.

'Joe, ask Mr Massinger to join us, will you?'

Joe went silently out of the room, without looking at M or assuming an expression. Gypsy shuffled from foot to foot and M said, with a sigh:

'Sit down, Fred.'

Gypsy took a seat on the edge of one of the cheap-looking chairs by the wall and sat with his knees apart and his hands dangling between them. Angela noticed that his right forefinger was heavily stained and guessed that if Gypsy had his way smoke would have been spiralling up between his knees. He winked at her and

53

she was annoyed to find herself looking primly away. To dissipate the impression she had at least given herself, she began to look round the room. The relief kept washing over her like a warm tide.

The room was without character. Desk, chairs, filing cabinets, white walls, and a blind. What did they add up to? Oh, to temporariness. They gave the impression that they would be gone tomorrow. Well, that was another of the true clichés. Tomorrow, M could be sitting in the back parlour of an osteopath, the next day above a betting shop.

The door opened and almost at once a hand came down on Angela's shoulder. She shuddered from the conditioning of recent hours even as she turned round in joyful expectancy and looked up into Gerald's face. She studied it anxiously, but it was as it had been when last she saw it, with the curl back in place. He was wearing a high-necked white pullover and what she thought must be uncharacteristically elderly grey trousers. He looked wonderful.

He said, smiling:

'You're all right now.'

'Oh, Gerald!'

'I'm afraid I wasn't able to keep you out of it.'

'You did your best. Oh, Gerald, I rang and rang!'

'I told you if I had the least suspicion they were still on my tail I'd go straight to the police station. One doesn't witness violent death every night.'

'No.' Angela shuddered again, turning back to M. 'When will you be able to . . . ?' She didn't know what to call it, and tailed off.

'Ah.' M fitted his finger-tips together. Gerald went and sat on the chair next to Gypsy, but leaning back and crossing his legs and making the chair look as if it was comfortable. 'You introduce the crux of the matter for me, Miss Canford. I cannot as yet, alas, say when we will—bring the matter to a conclusion. Although daily—hourly—we are in a better position for doing so, and for apprehending all those who are involved. In the meantime—they are desperate, and desperately dangerous. They still feel they can carry out their plans and escape our vigilance.'

'Gerald!' She swung round, but such was the weight of M's presence she turned back to him and excused herself before turning again to Gerald. 'Gerald, what about your friend, Guy wasn't it?'

Gerald looked at her, and it was the first time she had seen him hesitant.

'Gerald!'

Gerald looked over Angela's head at M, and Angela turned round to look at him, too.

'Miss Canford,' said M, very gently, 'Mr Massinger's friend was brave. He has—paid the penalty.'

'You mean'—she could hardly speak. M was nodding. 'You mean—he's dead?'

'Yes, my dear.'

'Was he working for you?'

'No. But chance—that same chance that led you into trouble, Miss Canford—gave him some information, and he "had a go" as they say, on his own stupidly courageous account.'

'Oh, Gerald!'

He was very pale. He said:

'You mustn't worry. There won't be any other small heroic deaths.'

'It is a question,' resumed M, 'of a few weeks.' He had buried Guy. 'We are confident. But during those weeks . . . Miss Canford, if you and Mr Massinger were to leave here and make for your homes, I do not think that either of you would reach them.'

The stab of fear that came then was worse than any that had gone before. Angela said, clutching the desk top:

'My parents!'

'So long as they know nothing,' said M gravely, 'and you are not with them, they will be safe.' Such was the weight of his presence, and the confidence with which he spoke, that Angela felt instantly reassured. 'We will, of course, keep careful though discreet watch on them.'

While she . . . Oh, she was an idiot. She had looked not one moment beyond the relief, the devastating relief, of now.

'And we? Gerald and I?'

Gypsy's voice said suddenly, so that she jumped:

'Photographs.'

She looked round at him. He didn't seem to have moved at all. This time, when she caught his eye, she didn't look away, she half smiled, but he merely went on staring at her so that she had to turn, at last, back to M.

M said:

'Ah, yes,' and opened a folder on his desk. He turned it round and pushed it across to Angela. It contained a few photographs of men's faces.

'Tell me if you've seen any of these before,' suggested M.

The photos were blown up, and seemed all to have been taken by flashlight. Angela turned them over reluctantly, not wanting to find what she found in the end. All the faces looked coarse, hard and angry, but only in the last one did she recognise the hostile eyes that seemed once again to stare into hers. She trembled and looked across at Gerald who made a half gesture towards her, smiling in concern, not uncrossing his legs.

'You recognise somebody?' asked M.

'This last one . . .' Angela tried to turn the file round, but her hands shook so much that all the photos slid out and got mixed up on the desk. Gypsy was suddenly there, putting them back.

'Which one?' pressed M.

'That one.'

Angela pointed, and Gypsy put the photograph she had pointed to on the top of the pile. He and M looked at it, then at each other for a moment. M turned back to Angela.

'Yes,' he said. 'Yes.' He leaned back in his chair, fitting his finger-tips together and sighing.

'Did you find—anything in the house?' Angela dropped her eyes as she spoke. They had found Guy's body, of course.

'Nothing—of any significance. The birds had flown. For these coming weeks, Miss Canford, before we finally—er— catch the thief'—M paused carefully—

'there is simply no alternative to your remaining under our protection.'

She and Gerald. She looked towards him. He was studying his knee, picking something infinitesimal off his trouser leg.

'You and Mr Massinger.'

She had wanted so much to see Gerald again, and now fate had given a macabre blessing to her longing, and had withdrawn the peace of mind in which she could have enjoyed it.

'How will I be able to make contact with my mother and father? And get some things?'

All she had was one crumpled tissue.

M went on, more gently than ever:

'You won't be able to make contact, Angela.' The use of her first name for the first time at this juncture was horribly impressive. 'You won't be able to see them or speak to them. For their sakes as much as your own. Nobody can fetch your things. Your house will be under constant watch from hostile eyes as well as protective ones. Do you want to lead the villains straight to us?' He held up his hand magisterially to check her reply. 'Your mother would be followed if she went out. Visitors to your father's office would be followed when they left. Do you understand?'

She did. Suddenly and completely, and her fear for her parents, and her longing to see them and comfort them, was stronger than anything else.

'Yes, oh, yes. But—they'll be all right. Oh, please . . .'

'I shall speak to them myself, Angela, and assure them of your safety—and their own.'

She couldn't speak or she would weep. She nodded her thanks. A swelling was growing in one corner of her mouth. M leaned over the desk and took hold of her hand in his wide white one. She realised how hot hers was, against the dry soft coolness of M's.

'You can give me any message you wish, the exact words of it, and I will pass it on to them. But we must permit no element of risk whatsoever. They might have managed to plant a device on your telephone. Special Branch does not claim a monopoly of electronic competence.'

'Yes. Yes, of course.' She made a desperate effort to pull herself together, venturing a shaky laugh.

'It's awful, isn't it, how dependent one becomes on things? The thought that I haven't any things at all with me—comb, nightie, purse, anything—you just take them for granted, you can't imagine living without them. Oh!'

'Without them,' said M solemnly, 'you will live.' He squeezed her hand and released it. He fitted his finger-tips together. 'We will see that you have everything you need.'

There was a pause. Angela's mouth throbbed. Gypsy shuffled his feet and coughed. Joe coughed. M began to stack papers together in a possibly dismissive gesture.

'Will I—we—stay here?' asked Angela, glancing at Gerald. He was still studying his trouser leg.

'Well, now,' said M, on a lighter note. 'What do you think about going to France?'

CHAPTER 4

'It is not, of course,' said M ponderously, 'simply a question of—er—getting on a train and going.'

He beamed at Angela over the desk, and she smiled back, uncomprehending but almost cheerful. It was morning, and although the venetian blind was pulled down, a brilliant sun still burst its imperfections here and there, stabbing the far wall with points of light. Angela felt well, for a start. She had fallen asleep almost as soon as she lay down in the narrow bed in the tiny bedroom, wearing the nightdress that had been laid out for her, having cleaned her teeth with the toothbrush provided and walked to and from the bathroom in the dressinggown that had been laid out with the nightdress.

There had been no book, and Angela couldn't remember the last time she had gone to sleep without reading (even the terrible night of the Bella Ball she had read a couple of pages of *Emma*). And without a book she was totally exposed to worries about her parents, which would attack her whatever M had said.

But her shuddery descent between cold sheets was followed immediately by a slight sound which made her sit upright, staring into the mild face of Sid who was standing there in his brown overalls, bearing a breakfast tray.

'Good morning, miss. Did you sleep well?'

'I died,' said Angela, then giggled nervously, in the circumstances. But Sid had gone, leaving a boiled egg, toast, and tea.

As she ate and drank, finding herself with an appetite, Angela was grateful for the swift transition from sleep to waking. How would she have felt, coming in the slow natural way back to consciousness, in those first moments when the instinctive contentment of waking gives way to memory?

As it was, the hot tea was a supporting rod in her chest. She was strong. And safe. And excited. She could just see her face in the mirror across the room, wide-eyed. And Gerald would be sitting over just such a tray, only the other side of a wall or two. Not in this flat, admittedly, the Branch had the one next door too, and that was Gerald's quarters.

There was no sound anywhere. Angela got out of bed, a piece of toast in her hand. The small window gave on to a well, blind except for a column of windows like her own, plunging down beneath her; when she stuck her head out she could just see their parallel lines moving inwards to a point far below, its end lost in darkness. This flat appeared to be a penthouse: blue sky, smudged with thin cloud, shone at her over the parallel flat roof.

Angela got back into bed as a knock sounded at the door. It must be a man, she was sure there was no woman in this strange retreat, cosy but comfortless.

She said 'Come in!' across a sensation of Gypsy's hand again on her mouth—a horrible yet compelling sensation—and thought she was relieved to see Sid. He advanced for the tray, said:

'Will you get up now, please,' and left her.

The sudden homesickness was an almost physical pain. She battled through the worst of it while she was dressing, and then Sid knocked again.

'Leave the bed,' he said, 'they're waiting for you.'

The words had an ominous sound to them, even in that anonymously safe place. If there were, for the moment, no bad men, there could still be bad news. In those long hours of the night, when she had slept so peacefully—so callously, she almost thought—the men guarding her home might have slept too.

'Sid!' Angela grasped the sleeve of his overalls. She thought he looked at her with sympathy. The overalls smelt of cooking fat and it might have been blood on the front of them. Last night he had served her a chop on a tray in the sitting-room.

'Speak to them,' said Sid. 'Come along.'

He led the way across the tiny hall. Angela, who had noticed so little in the daze of the night before, needed a guide. All doors were shut but for one that showed a glimpse of two single beds, very much unmade. She had started to wonder, as she fell asleep, who was in the flat with her. M had put on his coat and left before supper, Gypsy and Joe had watched her eat, and watched Gerald. Then Joe had taken Gerald away, out of the front door, and Gypsy had yawned and stretched, and left the room, and Sid had come and taken Angela across the hall as he was doing now. Gypsy and Sid in twin beds! Angela wanted to laugh, but the impulse, slightly hysterical, passed as quickly as it had come, and when Sid opened the office door she ran up to the desk—only later she realised that she had felt less inhibited in the absence of Gerald—and leaned over it, close to M's attentive face, noticing even in her singlemindedness the agreeable suggestion of his cologne.

'I'm terribly sorry but I'm so desperately worried about my parents it isn't that I don't trust you I've got complete faith of course but I would so like to speak to them myself just a word couldn't you . . .'

Damn. Damn. Damn. The struggle against tears had become so intense she couldn't say another word. She found herself sitting down under the slight pressure of Gypsy's hand on her shoulder. He and Joe were standing one each side of her.

'Angela,' said M, after a quick glance from Gypsy to Joe, 'listen.'

Angela nodded. It was still the only response she could make.

'I have spoken,' said M, 'to your parents this morning. All is well with them. The house is constantly under surveillance—by the police, you understand'—briefly he shook and rumbled—'and it has been decided that for the moment they will not leave it. Your father (like yourself) is diplomatically indisposed—there is a severe strain of influenza about. Your mother is having her shopping done for her—by us.'

M's gravity had never seemed so reassuring. 'We are confident,' he went on, 'that the—men involved will soon realise that the innocent intervention of yourself and Mr Massinger was a misfortune for them that they must carry on in despite of. In other words, the pressure on your parents, and on Mr Massinger's, can only slacken.'

'On Mr Massinger's!' repeated Angela, slowly and stricken. 'I never thought . . .'

Her wonderful relief was shot through with remorse.

'Well, perhaps not,' said M kindly. 'You have had enough to worry about on your own account.'

Angela saw a small frown appear between his eyes as he watched what she could feel as the persisting gloom of her face.

'France!' he said, so firmly that she yielded up the now inaccurate picture of her parents in danger to a vision of sand, sea and brown bodies. But how to reach it?

'Won't it be dangerous, leaving here—and going to France? Going anywhere?'

Was it only last night that she had entered this cocoon?

M smiled slightly, fitting his finger-tips together.

'You have no doubt heard the theory,' he said, 'that the best way to hide an object is to place it among a myriad similar objects.'

Angela thought Gypsy shuffled his feet. He had no doubt heard the theory.

'Pebbles,' said M, 'are the usual illustration. You want to steal my pebble, so I place it on the beach among billions of other pebbles. Can you find it?'

'Can *you?*' Angela was unable to resist the counter-question, and was relieved to see that it appeared to amuse M.

'Ah, no!' he said, with that same inward shake which the day before had preceded laughter. 'But pebbles are inanimate, they cannot say, when the right person comes along, "Here I am". You are not inanimate, Angela, nor Fred here, nor Joe, nor—other useful people. Therefore if we put you on the beach—and that is, literally, what we intend to do'—he shook again, briefly—'you will remain in the crowd merely for the short period of danger.'

'But—getting out of the country—surely they'll be waiting at airports, stations . . . ? They'll know!'

The men involved, who killed other men and had eyes like laser beams and fiendish intelligences, had almost, in Angela's mythology, acquired supernatural powers.

'Ah.' Once again M wore the satisfied air of one whose point has been made for him by his opponent. 'Allow me to introduce you.'

He twitched a piece of foolscap paper, on the desk in front of him, so that it faced Angela. It was neatly typewritten, in small paragraphs, and headed:

'Miss Caroline Mary Thompson.'

Angela read swiftly down. Miss Thompson was twenty-one years of age, lived in Richmond, had two parents living and a brother, had spent a couple of years on and off with a family in the Dordogne after leaving school.

'Richmond and the Dordogne,' said Angela, 'I know them well . . .'

'Read on,' said M gently, and Gypsy snorted, and Angela read that Miss Thompson and her family were about to set off for the South of France on holiday; they had hired a car, and after perhaps a week or ten days in Cannes they would carry on where fancy led them.

She was at the foot of the page, and when she flipped it over the back was blank.

She looked up at M. He was still gazing at her steadily, almost in compassion, it might have been, and on an instant she knew what they were going to do. She felt her face change.

M nodded. 'Yes,' he said, 'Miss Caroline Mary Thompson.' He made her a just perceptible bow. 'The young lady who will leave this flat in five days' time.'

'With her brother!'

'With her brother. And her mother and father. Joe, ask Sid for some coffee, will you? Miss Canford can absorb the idea while she drinks it.'

But the idea was already absorbed. It was as if Angela had always been privy to it. But there was one sharp thought.

'You said my parents were perfectly safe where they were.'

'So they are. And will remain. It is Caroline Thompson's parents with whom she will be travelling.'

'Oh!' She had not, after all, entirely understood.

'There is,' said M, as Sid came in behind a tray of coffee, followed by Joe who slid back into place, 'a great deal to be done.'

She was suddenly excited, eager. They went through the sheet of paper together, small item by small item. She was to remember that she was twenty-one, she was to learn, and remember, all the new facts about herself and suppress the old, *learn* them until they were part of her reflexes—'Yes, in five days'—but otherwise she was to behave naturally.

'Your natural behaviour,' said M gently, 'may, in any event, be somewhat—modified since the commencement of this unpleasant—affair.'

Oh, but it might. And meanwhile it was good to have some work to do again, and against a deadline, to whip energy and memory into line.

When M had taken her through the paper he went away, and Joe took her through it again, and added more type-written sheets with more small facts on them, and M returned and asked her if she had any questions, and some of her questions revealed that the list was still not quite long enough.

'You are a bright young lady,' said M, looking at Angela reflectively, and she only realised, when she looked round in triumph at Gerald, that he wasn't there, and that he hadn't been there all morning.

'Where's Gerald? He's got as much work to do as I have!'

M shook again, and Angela thought he must have been wondering how long it would take her to ask the question.

'Ah, yes,' said M, 'it has been decided that the—training sessions will be more effective if undertaken separately.'

'Ah, no!' But in a way she was relieved, sensing that she would get on better and faster without Gerald to witness any mistakes.

'Can we meet at meal times?'

'At dinner.'

And after dinner, tired, relaxed . . .

71

'And after dinner you will go to bed, because this is a time for work and you will be working very hard and will have to have an alert mind.'

'Yes, of course.'

Gypsy stuck his head round the door.

'Time!' he said.

It was one o'clock, to Angela's surprise.

They gave her some lunch on a tray in what Gypsy called the lounge, on an armchair which was part of a hideous three-piece suite of uncut moquette facing an empty tiled grate of the same pallid green as the marbled walls of the public stairway (was it only yesterday that she had seen it?). The carpet was in squares of russet and brown, the blind was down.

Joe sat with her, staring at the wall beside her head so that there was no conversation and Angela could prop up the typewritten sheets and think uninterrupted of Caroline and Caroline's life, as M had gently suggested would be a good habit to get into. Angela lamented Caroline's complete lack, at the age of twenty-one, of intellectual achievement, but had to admit that she, at eighteen, could hardly sustain the role of one who had just completed, or was about to complete, a university career.

'And,' as Gypsy said when she went back to the office in the afternoon, 'you don't paint, you haven't done one of those high-class secretarial nonsenses, you don't sing or play the joanna, you can't . . .'

'I get your point,' Angela interrupted, and Gypsy drew smoke in with a hiss (he smoked only when M was absent). 'What I meant was, people—perfect strangers—talk *interminably* about what they do. Anyway, if I could only say, "I wanted to go to university, but . . ." I'd be much more convincing. I know I would. Because otherwise I shall tend to despise Caroline, which wouldn't be a Good Thing. Oh, it's so hot, please, please open the window!'

Joe walked across the room, after a glance at Gypsy, and did this without disturbing the blind, and Gypsy said:

'You'd better ask Mr McGregor.'

'Who?'

'Mr McGregor. The boss.' He perhaps gave the word a mock emphasis. Angela felt disappointed.

But at least it began with an M.

So this was one of the questions she put to M when he came in a few minutes later.

'I shan't be so good if I feel entirely unlike myself,' she said earnestly. 'Not that'—suddenly embarrassed by M's thoughtful gaze, and the possibility that he might have a daughter who saw nothing to despise in herself for not having *intellectual aspirations*—'not that I'm trying to say everyone ought to go in for higher education—only that it's *me*, you see.'

'I do see,' said M, and he told Angela that she might confess to rheumatic fever and subsequent slight but now surmounted weakness of heart at the crucial time, and could cut down the length of her stay in the Dordogne.

'Oh, thanks!' She felt as if an understanding producer had recast her role. 'It'll be so much easier now, and easier will mean better, won't it?'

'Yes, young lady, easier will undoubtedly mean better. Tomorrow,' said M, 'Fred will give you the name of the doctor who treated you for the fever and subsequent heart condition, and will tell you how you felt.'

'You're so—small here,' said Angela, impressed to the point of comment, 'yet in touch with such—vast resources.'

Mentally she grinned, catching herself out in M's habit of punctuating his remarks with portentous pauses and using rather pompous words. It was fearfully contagious.

'Ah, yes,' said M, beaming, 'vast resources.'

'How's Gerald getting on? Doesn't he
have the benefit of your personal tuition?'

'I am not,' said M, 'with you all the
time, Angela. And I am going to leave you
now. A young woman called Carys—
pseudonymous of course, but you appreciate that—is coming to measure you for
clothes, and to do your hair. I want you to
study your notes while your hair is drying. We'll go over them again before dinner.'

Carys was brisk and attractive. She
brought shoes and handbags and a selection of make-up for Angela to choose from
(with her advice), and took her detailed
measurements. She washed Angela's hair
and afterwards, sitting down in front of
the dressing-table mirror, Angela had a
moment of panic when she saw scissors in
Carys's hand.

But Carys suddenly slowed down and
smiled radiantly at Angela's worried reflection and said, almost in her ear although they were alone in the room: 'It'll
be ever so much prettier as well as safer, I
promise you.'

So Angela concentrated on her notes,
trying to get used to the fact of living in
Richmond, of having a brother and of

being twenty-one, studying some rather blurry snapshots of her house and clearer ones of the surrounding areas, slightly dog-eared snapshots that she was to tuck into her new wallet when she felt they were familiar. So it wasn't until Carys came to brush out her hair that Angela saw it had been bleached a lot lighter and that it was quite short and an entirely different shape.

This was a shock, as real a physical shock as Gypsy's hand on her mouth in the wood, but at the moment the shock went through her, Angela was admitting, for the first time in her life, that her hair really looked quite nice. If it wasn't for her skin . . .

Angela pulled a face into the mirror. 'It really should have cleared by the time I'm twenty-one. It's adolescence, isn't it? I hope it's adolescence.'

'It'll clear,' said Carys, and slapped some lotion on Angela's face, and left the bottle for her, together with some cosmetics, a hairbrush and combs. She asked Angela what sort of clothes she liked, and Angela found she didn't really know.

'Will you leave it to me?' queried Carys, poised for departure.

'Oh, yes, oh, I wish you weren't going!' If Carys hadn't come at all, perhaps Angela wouldn't have realised how much she missed a woman in the flat. But there was an excitement in turning back to the mirror when Carys had gone. And her skin, that would have to clear, because Angela could only think of Caroline, even while doubting her intelligence, as an enviably sophisticated creature who couldn't possibly suffer from a bad skin . . .

Sid knocked at the door and asked her to step into the lounge. M was there, smiling expansively against the blind which now obscured a gentler light.

'My dear Caroline,' he said, twinkling, 'how nice you look!'

Before she had time to really enjoy the compliment there was a sound behind her, and she whirled round. Gerald was in the doorway. It seemed to Angela so long since she had seen him that she had forgotten the impact of his perfection. She hoped he might approve the drastic change to her head, but he had no visible reaction. Admittedly his eyes were on her, but they held no expression.

'Let us,' said M, *co-ordinate.*'

He sat down in the centre of the sofa, waving his hands to the two dreadful flanking chairs. Angela and Gerald sat down. Gerald's face was calm and intent.

'Peter,' said M pleasantly, turning

slightly towards Gerald, 'how on earth did you wangle—what is it?—two, three weeks off like this?'

Gerald looked amused, took his time.

'We don't all work in offices, you know. I haven't wangled anything, I'm afraid, unless it's a situation in which it's terribly hard to make myself get down to it . . .'

'So you're not really on holiday? You're working?' Angela noticed that M's eyebrows, as they rose side by side, had the same reddish tinge that the late sun was giving to the top of his hair, where a furry shaft of sunbeam struck it on the way to the wall.

'Well, without pressure. I'm just between finishing researching a book and starting to write the wretched thing—so perhaps I'm due a bit of a holiday.'

'Do tell us,' pursued M, 'what it's about!'

Gerald raised both hands, with a deprecating smile.

'I'm so very sorry,' he said, 'that I can't oblige you. I just never do, at this stage. It tends to make it all blow away.'

'Who's your publisher?' Angela asked, realising only after she had spoken that her interest in the ingenious situation had overtaken her diffidence, even her awe of Gerald's sophistication.

This time Gerald's eyebrows went up, one fractionally in front of the other. M said, smiling:

'You'll avoid people who are likely to ask that question.'

'Yes, but, can we be sure we'll be able to avoid them?'

'No,' said Gerald, looking at Angela, 'although one has instincts.'

'Yes, and normally, they'd be the people one wanted to talk to. But honestly,' Angela turned to M, 'someone might ask me who publishes my brother.'

'You can never remember the name,' said M.

'Does it exist?'

'Something very like it. Do you know this part of France, Caroline?' asked M, switching his attack.

'No, I don't.' She found this latest lurch of the heart as exciting as a roller coaster.

'But your parents have been here before?'

'Oh, yes—and when it was much more attractive, as they're always telling me.'

'What are you going to do when you get home?'

'Oh, don't ask me, *I* don't know!' said Caroline. 'How I hate saying that!' said Angela, and thought that Gerald's mouth twitched at the corner. But M said, coldly (and coldness from M was chill indeed):

'I am addressing Caroline.'

It was a nasty shock, but even before she had absorbed it M was playful again.

'It's quite refreshing these days to hear of a young woman who hasn't got loads of plans to *do* things. But I don't believe you, Caroline!'

'Well, I'm telling you.'

'Is there perhaps'—archness suited M far better than chill—'a—reason?'

Angela, warned, gave full scope to her conception of Caroline, who tossed her head—'odious bridling', thought Angela—and said she didn't know, again. But M went wheedling, and she knew she must move to the next lesson.

'Take a secretarial course, I suppose,' she said, sighing. 'I've been putting it off for much too long as it is.'

'Where will you go?'

'Do you mind? I haven't got *that* far!'

M leaned back, looking at her thoughtfully. To her surprise she saw that Gerald was smiling.

'That's very good,' said M, 'you've made a very good start. You are intelligent, Caroline.'

'Not Caroline! Angela!' Her indignant voice rang in her ears, and Gerald's smile broke into a laugh, the first real laugh Angela had heard from him, and rather too high-pitched to match the rest of his beauty.

M and Angela both turned to him.

'With respect, sir,' said Gerald, and Angela fancied she saw his choice of words, his soft tone, as a deliberate small mark of disrespect, 'the lady is right. It is Angela who is intelligent and who despises Caroline because she has the idea that Caroline is less so. Such an opinion between the two women could be—well, I think it could be unfortunate.' He looked at Angela. 'You don't think much of Caroline, do you? Why?'

She could hardly suppress the delight that flooded her at his praise of Angela. 'She—she hasn't done anything. Oh, I know you've let me have an explanation for that'—she gave M a hasty grateful smile—'but she isn't wanting to do anything. She has no views.'

'Some dramatist said somewhere,' murmured Gerald, 'that doing was a flight from being. It wouldn't do Angela any harm to ponder that.'

'Well—yes. Up to a point. But you must have views.'

'So give them to Caroline,' said Gerald,

suddenly impatient, 'and come to terms with her.'

He was right, of course. She was inventing a problem, it must be out of that intellectual arrogance that Simon had hinted at years and years ago in the Playhouse foyer. Certainly, she could put Caroline over well enough.

Angela wished M would speak. The cheap clock on the tile mantelpiece seemed to crescendo its hurried ticking. Angela heard her stomach, in the silence, ask softly for its supper.

'Well, child,' said M at length, 'can we take it that you have absorbed Mr Massinger's advice?' It seemed to Angela that he and Gerald exchanged glances. She burst out:

'You think I'm a prig!'

Was she?

'On the contrary,' said M soothingly, 'I think you are doing very well indeed, as I have already told you, and what Mr Massinger thinks is of no importance'— here came one of his characteristic pauses—'to this enterprise.'

Gerald's face had flamed brilliant red in an instant, and Angela thought, he doesn't normally get correction, he isn't used to it. She looked away from him. He would not wish to be taken so unawares in front of her. And besides, it didn't suit him.

At dinner he was his calm pale self. Tired, she thought, as she was. Gypsy made a third with them. At first Angela tried to start a few topics of conversation, but lapsed through lack of support. But she still found the meal interesting because of the dramatic contrast between the two men: both so handsome, one in a familiar idiom that attracted and the other in a fierce almost outrageous way that repelled—one of course from her world, and one at home everywhere and nowhere. The hound and the fox, perhaps. Animal images kept cropping up when she contemplated Gypsy. . .

Gypsy drained his coffee cup, pushed his chair away from the table by pressing his legs against the table legs, yawned and stretched.

'So now the day is over and Miss Thompson retires.'

'And Mr Massinger?' asked Angela, irritable in her disappointment. Even though M had ordained an early bed, she had not seen it as quite so defeating of all possibility of post-prandial relaxation with Gerald.

'And Mr Massinger,' agreed Gypsy, 'and self. We're all working tomorrow.'

A sudden thought filled her with dismay.

'But I've nothing to read. I can't go to sleep without something to read.'

She really didn't think that she could. That first night had been the exception of a lifetime. She looked, instinctively and foolishly, at Gerald, who could do nothing for her. As it was, he raised one eyebrow and smiled slightly, while Gypsy said, 'Sorry, doll.' Angela found herself getting to her feet and saying:

'Goodnight, then.'

Gerald half left his chair for an instant. He said:

'Relax. You'll go straight to sleep.'

'Will you?' She heard the anger in her voice and felt tears far down.

'I shall hope to. We need our strength, Angela Caroline.'

'I know.' She wasn't angry, only tired. 'Goodnight, then.'

Gerald half rose a second time. Now choking down an impulse to laugh hysterically, Angela wondered how often she could make the little scene re-enact itself. But she walked out, across the tiny hall, into her bedroom.

Someone had drawn the curtains, turned on the bedside light, and removed the bedspread. Angela had been expecting to give herself up, as soon as she was alone, to her hovering melancholy, picturing the unlit room with its square of dusky window as the setting, but these small preparations for her night were sufficient to banish it completely. Instead of being miserable she was excited. When she came out of the bathroom Gypsy was standing at her door and said:

'What big eyes you've got!'

Angela had noticed them too, staring at her from the mirror.

'Thanks—whoever it was—for drawing my curtains and so on.'

'Sid's always had a strong sense of hospitality.'

Gypsy in the half-light was less brutally attractive. His tobacco smell, mingled with some other smell, almost a scent, made her think of France. She realised she was slightly out of breath.

'You can have this,' said Gypsy. He held out an untidy newspaper.

'Thanks. Oh, thanks!'

It was the *Daily Mirror*. Angela clutched it gratefully and fled into her room. Her gratitude was for the gesture rather than the gift, but she found herself smiling over a couple of cartoons and a scandalous news item. If she read a newspaper it was usually the *Times* or the *Telegraph*.

What would Caroline read? Probably the *Daily Express* . . .

Angela kicked her legs irritably about the bed. Why did she keep on thinking of Caroline as a person whose identity she was usurping rather than creating, a person with a character, with tastes, already formed? It was for Angela to say what Caroline liked reading, how she reacted.

Angela threw the *Daily Mirror* on the floor and picked up some of the Caroline biographical notes. It was good to have work to do, something with which she was obliged to occupy her mind. But she was, once more, beautifully, uncomplicatedly, tired. In a few minutes she turned the light off and lay down. She postponed thinking about her mother and father, and fell asleep as she was looking, in the dim light that came through the thin curtains, at the outline of Caroline's cosmetic jars on the dressing-table.

— CHAPTER 5 ———————

As they sat down to dinner the third night—Angela, Gerald and Joe—Gerald put a book on the table beside Angela's plate. It was a thick paper-back, Mrs Gaskell's *Wives and Daughters*. He said:

'It's oddly absorbing.'

'Gerald . . .' Angela thought she had never been more pleased.

'I asked Joe.'

Angela looked across at Joe, already stolidly eating. The mental picture of Joe entering W. H. Smith and Son and asking for *Wives and Daughters* by Mrs Gaskell struck her as so ludicrous that she choked on her first mouthful. With laughter. Or was she crying? She was very tired.

Gerald told her to take it easy, but she had to tell him how kind he had been.

'I only asked Joe.'

'But you asked him.'

Gypsy was absent that evening, and when Angela and Gerald weren't talking there was silence. They didn't talk very much. Joe ate steadily, seemingly absorbed in his food—so that it was frightening the way his hand was at his pocket almost instantaneously with a crash from the hall, and it was only a second or two later that he was at the door. Sid's face came round it in mild apology, into the muzzle of Joe's gun, which he ignored.

'I dropped that cursed copper bowl. Sorry. Sorry, miss.'

Joe sat down again and picked up his knife and fork. Angela said, shakily:

'A dummy run like that is awfully reassuring.'

Gerald smiled briefly and politely into his plate, and Angela looked with admiration at his pale profile, appreciating its perfection. It gave her the sort of pleasure she got out of certain pictures, or beautiful ideas.

'How are you getting on with Peter, Gerald?'

Joe took a second helping of potatoes. Sid was a good cook.

'I think perhaps—I'm not having the same problem that you are. I don't find anything to despise in Peter. I rather envy him, as a matter of fact—the chap's making it all round.'

He was teasing her, which she rather liked. Sid came in as Joe finished his last mouthful and took their plates away. He gave them each a small bowl very full of apple pie and custard.

'Oh, I envy Caroline in some ways too!' said Angela, rather to her own surprise. Gerald raised one eyebrow.

'In what ways?'

'I don't know, really. I suppose—because she's more sophisticated than Angela, takes things more easily, doesn't get so het up.' Was she teasing, too? She really didn't know. 'I'm talking nonsense, perhaps. But I see Caroline a certain way. I can't help it. Even where it ought to be me. But none of her seems up to me, somehow. She already existed . . .'

Angela stopped, realising that Gerald was looking at her continuously and without reserve, as if suddenly his instinct told him there was no longer any need to hold her at arms' length. But she hadn't changed. Perhaps it was just that he had decided it could be less draughty if he recognised his friend in need.

Sid brought coffee in, as he had done the night before. Already to Angela, that third evening, the routine of the flat, so strict, so simple, felt as if it had been going on for ever. She had always known the thirties decor of the lounge, the little pointed mushroom salts, the table mats with their scratched views of London, the smell of Gypsy's tobacco (even when he wasn't there), the hardness of the office chairs, and the pneumatic itch of the un-cut moquette, where she and Gerald sat down in the evening with M before dinner, to be tested on the day's progress.

There were to be changes, of course, shifts of emphasis as the days reproduced themselves. Angela ceased to protest against Caroline's flippancies, instead she gave them an increasingly consistent rendering and M grew consistently more satisfied. She enjoyed the process more and more. She hardly read at night, hardly worried, before falling into a dreamless sleep. She was always dog-tired. She enjoyed the idea of Gerald as her brother, to her surprise. But since that third evening she knew their relationship had undergone an improvement, if not the improvement she had at first dreamed of and longed for.

But the real change, through those five identically ordered days, was the growth in Angela's knowledge of Caroline Thompson, reinforced by the fresh items of clothes and accessories which she found almost every time she went into her bedroom.

It was a knowledge not easily won. Gypsy could be cruel, lashing her with his tongue, shouting, threatening to strike her even, then lending her his handkerchief if she cried. It had an uneasy scent to it.

Joe was as persistent, quietly, and frightened her more. Both of them worried over and over again at the same points, sent questions across like a hail of bullets, shifted ground (physically sometimes, so that she whipped round like a baited animal), tried to trick her and catch her out. It amazed her that she went each morning into the office tense with excitement rather than with fear, knowing as she did what strains the day would bring. But Angela found that she enjoyed marshalling her forces to meet the attack, enjoyed feeling her brain drawn out like an aching muscle, enjoyed even the anger to which they goaded her sometimes with their own rage and contempt against her, enjoyed building up Caroline like a Galatea, learning a personality, not merely a set of apparent facts. The sessions with M and Gerald were even more exciting. Perhaps she was an actress *manquée?* This possibility was exciting too—she had never till this moment considered that she could do anything with any skill which demanded more than her brain.

At the end of the afternoon session on the fifth day, Gypsy got up from the chair he had straddled while he was questioning her, flopped down in M's big chair behind the desk, swivelled it a complete round and said:

'We're there, doll!'

'I can't believe it!'

'But you do believe it!' Gypsy grinned at her through his smoke. Joe, his task done, stood silent, expressionless as ever.

'Yes, I suppose so. I know I shan't make mistakes now, it's become reflex. But five days ago . . .'

'You don't measure progress by days, doll.'

Oh, she knew that. Because sometimes just one minute could be . . .

'You're all rosy. Joe, open the window.'

Angela pushed her hair back from her damp forehead. 'It's the effort. Are you really satisfied with me, Gypsy?'

Gypsy's smile widened as it always did when Angela used her name for him. 'I'm satisfied with you, doll.'

When she went to her room, to titivate before the meeting with M (she did this every evening since Carys had sent her into the lounge with her new hair style), Angela found three matching and elegant suitcases, and when she went through into the lounge she found M waiting beside a silver tray that contained glasses and a decanter of sherry. It was the first time she had seen alcohol since her lifetime in the flat had begun, although she thought she had smelled it on Gypsy and Joe sometimes during the afternoon sessions.

The sherry marked a change in the routine which must, in this world of continuous significance, have a meaning. Angela was suddenly afraid.

M said, at his most benevolent:

'Well, now . . .' and poured her a glass of sherry. Angela saw her hand tremble as she took it, and the next second the doorbell shrilled so that a small wave of sherry gushed up and over the edge of the glass, on to the carpet. It sank without trace. With undimmed smile M murmured:

'I knew there would have to be something in favour of this carpet,' and then Sid ushered a man and a woman into the room.

Although Angela had never met Mother and Father, she knew a great deal about them and had seen a number of photographs. So she recognised them instantly. The woman small and neatly plump, her face at the same time sharp and fleshy. Discontented in repose, but unexpectedly attractive when smiling, perhaps because the teeth were good and well-shaped. Sallow complexion. Fair hair so subdued with bleach and perm that it would never get out of place. Well-schooled but not quite well-bred, Angela suddenly suspected, for no other reasons than a dislike of the heavy perfume and the inflection—was it a carefulness?—of the light, girlish voice. And perhaps a sort of defensiveness in the eyes. Angela had been wondering, of course, whether Mother and Father were Special Branch officers assuming their roles in order to protect her and Gerald. Or whether they, too, needed to lie low. It was impossible to tell.

Father was thin and dark and spectacled and unremarkable—average features, average height, average rather flat tones. But Angela thought she might come to like him better than Mother.

She scarcely had time to register her reactions before the woman bore down on her and took her fussily into her arms, crying 'Caroline!' and looking at her with cold bright eyes. Angela, making a dab with her lips at the yellow-brown cheek that was beside hers, said:

'Hello, Mother.'

The 'Mother' was a concession she had won from M by insisting she could never say 'Mummy'.

'Splendid!' murmured M, smiling widely, and Caroline's mother propelled the girl towards the man. Angela said 'Father' and their cheeks came together. He took her hands and said, 'Let's have a look at you,' then stepped back smiling slightly, and Angela managed to smile and say:

'How do you think I'm looking?'

'Very well!' answered M for Father, coming forward with glasses of sherry for Mr and Mrs Thompson.

The conversation, which was in character and mostly about the coming trip, was rather awkward and riddled with silences. Angela noticed that her parents either avoided looking at her, or slipped her the odd speculative glance, and then realised she was doing the same thing with them. The only acknowledged look she exchanged was with Gypsy, when he winked at her. After a few minutes Gerald came in, and Mother bore down on him, and he saluted Father and was made to stand beside Angela so that it could be seen what a fine young couple they were. Angela stretched out her hand the fraction necessary to touch Gerald/Peter's hand, and Gerald curled his little finger round hers in an unexpected gesture which was more comforting than anything her imagination could have devised. Mother's sallow cheeks flushed up as she looked at them and she gave a sharp cough. Gerald shifted slightly. Angela felt sorry and uncomfortable for him in the part he had to play: he was, after all, the man whose impact was in his dignity and sophistication. It was demeaning for him to be forced into this ridiculously inappropriate role. Yet Gerald kept a sort of good-humoured distance from his situation, he would not let himself be affected by it. Angela admired, among so much else, his continuing *sang froid*.

M seemed highly pleased, as at a successful fulfilment. He motioned the Thompson family to sit down. Second sherries were poured, and even Joe was brought forward for a moment into the benevolent spotlight, with a personal tribute by M to his part in the campaign. Angela noticed the sweat on his pale temples as he looked down at the floor. Gypsy took his compliments with a slick return, and Angela found herself with a strange feeling of disappointment, almost as if she was disappointed in Gypsy for being what he was, for not being . . . The overhead light was too bright and harsh and concentrated. Angela was desperately tired. She remembered lying in the soil inside the gates of home, too weary without great effort to struggle to her feet.

The gates of home. Mummy and Daddy.

The agonising pain of homesickness, which had been biding its time, assailed her again.

'Caroline!'

Jumping guiltily, Angela realised that the name had been called twice. There was a crease between M's brows and Mother's mouth was pursed. The homesickness must be postponed. Angela, who was surprising herself by the versatility of her instinct for self-preservation, avoided Gypsy's teasing eyes and said:

'I'm sorry about that, but please don't worry. I wander off sometimes, and just now I'm more tired than I've ever been in my whole life. I wouldn't have heard the other name either.'

They all laughed exaggeratedly at this, and M said the party was over and dinner must be served so that Caroline could get to bed as soon as possible.

'I give you,' he said pompously, above the last of his sherry, 'the demise—for the time being—of Gerald and Angela.' There was a murmur all round. On cue, everybody drained his or her glass. 'This moment,' went on M portentously, 'sees the entry on stage of Caroline and Peter.'

There was nothing to be said in answer to this pronouncement. Mother picked up her handbag and pecked the cheeks of the children. She and Father left with M. Joe went too. As the door closed Angela turned silently to Gerald with her arms wide and he took hold of her and whirled her round before setting her gently back on the sofa. Sid came in to lay the table.

'Cheer up!' said Gypsy, who had been watching and grinning. 'I'm coming with you, Car-o-line.' He pronounced the name in three distinct syllables. He flung himself into one of the moquette armchairs and addressed the ceiling through smoke and smoke rings.

'Finished packing?'

'I haven't started. But don't worry.' Angela felt somehow confused.

'Oh, I shan't,' said Gypsy. Angela's cheeks were hot. She had a headache.

'When do we leave?'

'In the morning. Not too early.'

Angela didn't sleep well, although she was more tired still when she had packed all her fine new things. She kept dreaming of journeys that went wrong, journeys that were never completed, involuntary journeys undertaken just over the borders of sleep—journey after journey begun and never ended, because the car was flagged down, or flint-faced men invaded the cabin, or the carriage was derailed, or suddenly she had no identity, falling between two identities, falling in a whirl-pool round and round, down and down, before the shocked eyes of Angela and Caroline (Angela was dark and Caroline fair and they were not alike), until it was so unbearable she must scream herself awake.

She lay rigid, hoping desperately that nobody had heard her, relaxing gradually into the continuing silence. It was still dark, although enough day had begun for her to see the shape of her travelling coat hanging behind the door. Angela began to pray: 'Dear God, sustain and comfort Mummy and Daddy.' She stopped, clasped her hands together, and began again: 'Dear God . . .'

Special Branch was a more reassuring phrase than Dear God. That was wrong. But Special Branch was under God, that was right . . .

'Miss,' said Sid, 'Miss, you are asleep, and no mistake.'

He was carrying the usual tray. There was a low grey sky and a few raindrops diagonal on the window pane.

'I haven't been asleep for long,' said Angela, sitting up. Sid smiled at her kindly. Mummy would probably give him a tip. Angela suppressed a giggle.

'All right, miss?'

'Oh, yes, Sid, yes.' She was, now, entirely all right, freed from the anticipatory terrors of her dreams. Tense and wary, though. Excited. 'Thanks for looking after me. So well.'

'Been a pleasure, miss.' Sid bustled out of the room.

Angela ate her breakfast quickly and sprang out of bed. The flat was silent, she met nobody on her way to and from the bathroom, but when she was ready and trying to disguise a spot on her chin, the doorbell rang. Mother's voice in the hall was unmistakable.

M said goodbye solemnly to Angela, while Sid took the cases downstairs. He held her hand for a long time, pumping it up and down. Joe stood by, and Angela sought his hand at his side, to say goodbye. It rested limply in hers. Strange to think of it tensing so quickly round a gun. Gypsy was nowhere to be seen, although his tobacco was about.

'I'm sorry to go,' said Angela laughing, 'I really am.'

'Of course,' said M gravely, 'this is your place of birth. This is the first time you have left home, Caroline. Take great care.'

'I will, Uncle Mac.' Terror had touched her again with his words.

'All aboard!' said Father.

'We'll see you, then?' asked Mother of M, in her soft light voice.

'You will.'

'And Gypsy and Joe?' asked Angela.

'You will see them too.'

Angela hesitated, then put her hand on M's arm. 'Mummy and Daddy?' she murmured.

'I have spoken to them this morning,' said M, smiling at her kindly, 'and they are well. They know you are safe. So are they.'

'Thank you!' She leaned up and kissed his cheek. As if to celebrate the rocketing of her spirits, Gerald was in the doorway, smiling at her too. They went down in the small claustrophobic lift. It was raining. Angela thought, today for the first time no sun would have come through the blinds, it's a sign, the journey had to begin. Nevertheless she shivered in the open air, feeling vulnerable, regretting the cocoon.

The car was there and they climbed in quickly. A new car this time, clean and shining. Gerald sat in the front beside Sid, who drove. He had abandoned his overalls for a pullover and grey slacks. Angela was between Mother and Father in the back.

They travelled in silence. Angela broke it once, early on, with an exclamation, when she realised where she had been. It was not very far from home. Homesickness tugged again, but sternly she repelled it.

They stopped twice on the way to Folkestone. Once by the roadside to eat the sandwiches and drink the coffee Sid had prepared for them. Once to use garage loos. The silence, of four tense people unable to share each others' thoughts, was utterly unlike the comfortable silences in which Angela travelled with Mummy and Daddy.

Mother sat back in the corner of the car, but her perfume took possession of the whole interior. Angela wondered which would win in a straight fight between Mother's perfume and Gypsy's tobacco. She sensed a particular tension in the woman, despite the negligence of her pose, and the fact that she frequently closed her eyes and appeared to doze. Father hardly moved.

Sid drove fast, and they were seldom held up. Landscape, towns, were colourless under the low grey sky. Angela watched, turn and turn about, the scene through the window (she was glad Sid drove fast, because she found herself flinching each time a car overtook them), and Gerald's pale profile. She must even, incredibly, have eventually fallen asleep, because when Father said 'Won't be long, now' it fitted into a dream she was having in which someone was trying to pick a lock.

Angela took her passport out and looked at the assurance of Her Britannic Majesty's Principal Secretary of State for Foreign Affairs and the photograph of Caroline staring from under her short fair hair. The photo had been taken by Carys, as soon as Angela's hair was brushed out. The passport, issued in London in the name of Caroline Mary Thompson, was valid for ten years. Well, Caroline wouldn't be renewing it. Angela hoped she might, in that far off time when significant things turned into souvenirs, be allowed to keep the passport. They could cut the corner off it as they cut the corners off honest passports when they went out of date . . .

'Caroline!'

Angela lurched back to the car and the woman beside her putting a small neat hand over hers.

'Yes, Mother?'

'We'll just take it easy now, dear, and not draw attention to ourselves.'

'Yes, Mother.'

So this was it. As they climbed out of the car Angela's acrobatic heart was in her throat. She half expected to hear, or feel, a shot, but without incident they joined a queue waiting to go through passport control. Sid walked slowly to and from the car carrying their cases, which he stacked beside them. He left them, with a salute, in the hands of a porter. It was drizzling.

It seemed like a long wait. Other people in the queue besides Angela were shivering, the damp wind drove in at the open sides of the shed. Men in the uniforms of policemen, customs officers, motoring organisations, strolled about, sometimes glanced at them. Idly, it seemed. Angela found she was saying to herself, over and over again: 'I am. While I can say I am, I am. Dear God. Nothing has happened to us. I am. I am here . . .'

'Your passport, please, madam.'

The man at the window was handsome and very young. He smiled at Angela as she handed him her passport. She wondered if he would have called her madam if she had not turned into Caroline. Suddenly she couldn't remember Mother's Christian name. She couldn't remember her own middle name. She couldn't remember anything. The top of the man's uniform hat looked sticky with drizzle. Another young man, hatless and in a light suit, was standing beside him. He looked down at some papers he held in his hand, then back at her, smiling. He even blushed.

'Going on holiday, are you?'

'That's right.'

She wondered at the lightness of her voice. Mother and Father were sauntering ahead, Gerald was behind her. Her heart was so loud she could hardly hear what the man said.

'Looking for something?' asked Gerald, with a grin.

'Oh, we're always looking for something, sir,' said the man in the light suit, apologetically. He turned back to Caroline, smiling admiringly. 'Where are you off to, then?'

'Cannes for a start,' said Caroline, 'then whither we will.' The pause had been so fractional she hoped she had been the only one to notice it. 'Would you like to carry our bags?'

It was astonishing to find how she relished these moments of potential danger, rose to them when they came even though she cowered in anticipation. She would never have believed it. But this man surely represented safety. He must be another agent of Special Branch, seeing them safely and unobtrusively on their way. He was as self-effacing as Joe, in a more attractive way. Of course, she felt the temptation to believe he was talking to her because of her *beaux yeux*, but Angela's pessimism and commonsense made her reject the notion almost as soon as it presented itself.

'Today, yes, I should like to carry your bags,' said the man, glancing out on the weather, 'but it's been lovely here just lately, hasn't it?'

'Lovely!' agreed Angela, remembering the stabs of light on the wall of the flat, and her longing for the sun that was shining.

'Thank you, sir, thank you, madam.' The passport officer gave them back their passports. 'Have a good time,' said the man in the light suit, with a last admiring glance at Caroline, turning back to his papers. They followed Mother and Father up the gangway and on to the ship.

It was raining in earnest now, and it was good in every way to be on board. A steward advanced on them outside the saloon door, and Angela hoped no one noticed her start of alarm. The steward said:

'Tea and toast!'

They went into the saloon and sat down at a table for four. Angela was curious to find out what pattern of behaviour was to emerge for mealtimes, and for all the other times when they would be on show as a family. She was also hungry and thirsty.

Peter began by drawing unflattering attention to the amount of jam Caroline helped herself to. She retorted out of a real small annoyance, genuinely stung him, too, she thought, then calmed him down on his counter-attack. The parents offered a few mildly corrective interjections. The process took them comfortably to the end of the meal. Angela thought it was quite a convincing pattern as far as eavesdroppers were concerned, and quite a pleasantly sustainable one. And it meant that she and Gerald were talking, even if in code, that they were needing each other the whole time for their mutual safety.

Mother lit a cigarette when all the toast was gone. Gerald said he was going up on deck and did Caroline want to come too. Angela looked curiously at the parents to see their reactions but Mother merely nodded, eyes narrowed against her smoke, and Father said:

'Good idea. Might see you up there myself, later.'

The feeling of excitement, scrambling up the steep stairway behind Gerald, was so strong it took over from every other sensation—fear, exhaustion, undercurrent thoughts of home.

The air that met her at the top was an expression of her mood. Angela stood at the rail, leaning on it, breathing deeply, feeling the breeze move through her short hair, then turned to Gerald in a sort of triumph.

'You look better,' he said judicially, studying her.

'I feel better.'

The water of the Channel was palest blue, the sky was palest blue, all the rainclouds were banished to the low horizon.

'Why is it so much easier for you, I wonder?' murmured Angela, almost to herself, but Gerald at once answered her.

'How do you know that it is?'

'I don't *know*. I just feel it.'

'This is not the sort of conversation we must have,' said Gerald, 'even when we think we're alone. If the family is to convince other people, and ourselves, we must live it every single moment.'

'You're right, of course.'

She looked at him with an apologetic smile, and was surprised at the sudden sadness in his face. She had never seen anything like it there before.

There was nothing to alarm them when they disembarked at Calais, but Angela was glad when she saw Father lock the door of their couchette. The night was hot and she was restless, tossing in the narrow bunk above Gerald. In the end she clicked on her small light and found that, as he had suggested, she could half-forget her own situation in the leisured rural past of Mrs Gaskell's novel, recalled to the present only by the occasional deep snort from Mother, lying across from her on her back. Father lay all night like a log. Angela wondered how well they knew one another, he and Mother, how they would lie when they were alone together as they must be in Cannes. She fell asleep at last with vaguely erotic thoughts—Caroline thoughts she called them, in her last conscious moment.

In the glorious golden morning, in Cannes, a car was waiting for them at the station. Father took the wheel and drove them to their hotel on the Croisette.

— CHAPTER 6 ————————

Angela wiggled bare toes in fine yellow
sand, nestling her body more comfortably
into the hired mattress. She was so near
the quiet sea that when she laid her head
on her arms and looked along to the left
she saw the edge of it telescope with the
promenade into a fine point which seemed
to pierce the picturesque buildings front-
ing the harbour at the foot of Le Suquet.
Le Suquet, Gerald had told her, was the
name for the mound of haphazard old
houses at the west end of the bay, crowned
with ancient churches.

It was an entrancing sight, insubstantial
in the shimmer of the heat haze, broken
intermittently by the bobbing heads of
children in and out of the water. Angela
sighed, with the nearest approach to contentment she had felt for what seemed a
very long time. She was almost dry from
her second swim of the morning. The sun
was hot on her shoulders and the backs of
her legs, but tempered by a small breeze.

And M had promised her that Mummy and Daddy would be safe . . .

She was, however, developing a crick in the neck. Angela turned her head the other way, thinking of the eastern curve of Cannes bay, the rocky outline of the modern Port Canto and the promontory beyond, crowned without rivalry to Le Suquet by the ornate cream palace of the summer casino. But her new horizon was the curve of Mother's stomach, rising and falling rhythmically in sleep.

Angela turned over and sat up. She looked with an unfamiliar sensation of approval down her legs, which were browning nicely, to her feet, which she had manicured in red in deference to Caroline's taste. She had realised while doing it that she had rather attractive feet. Mother's feet, on a level with Angela's calves, were not attractive, they were short and broad with a painful-looking bunion on each, and pearl pink toenails.

Angela looked with narrowed eyes across the fierce pale sparkle of the water. The Esterel mountains, opposite, were the vaguest of shadows. The air smelt of sun oil and flowers and Gauloises, and drowned even Mother's perfume. A breeze moved the edge of the large blue umbrella above Mother, and the shade of the fringe riffled across her nose. There was no horizon between pale blue sky and sea.

All round them were voices—male, female, grave, gay, old and young. Angela thought they were rather like birdsong in the spring—some excited, some admonitory, some repetitive (a negro crying sugared almonds, striding with long regular steps between the rows of bodies, his brown back glistening), some lyrical (soft French phrases from a concerned mother), some plaintive ('*Maman, quelle heure est-il?*'). The constant noise of cars from the Croisette above formed a background hum.

Angela closed her eyes again and nestled back, luxuriously, savouring the sun and the human music. Occasionally mother punctuated it with a snore, but however quickly Angela opened her eyes and looked at her, she was always still fast asleep.

Yet even in unconsciousness Mother's face seemed set in lines of unease, the mouth still drawn tight, the nose pointed aggressively upwards between the rather puffy cheeks. There was something lifeless about the skin as well as the hair—which made it dramatically noticeable the times that Mother blushed. The sun didn't appear to be having the slightest effect on her skin, although this was the third morning that Angela had come down with her to the beach, gone with her into the sea, even held her up under the water in an attempt (unsolicited and unsuccessful) to teach her to swim, then sat down beside her to dry and eventually (as now) watched her arrange the umbrella over the upper part of her face and sink into sleep. Nor did exposure to Angela's company appear to have had any effect on Angela's knowledge of her. Mother had, of course, where necessary, borne out the things that Angela had been taught during the sessions in the flat, but these had told her nothing about the woman's temperament and she was still no more to Angela than a few pages learned by heart.

Well (Angela, with a smile, threw back a large multi-coloured ball which had landed on her stomach), that was as it should be, it meant Mother was doing what she had been taught to do, what was wise. But although Angela attempted to respond as meagrely, she suspected that, even as Caroline, she was telling Mother far more about herself than she would ever begin to learn in return.

The whole extraordinary set up, though, did make life surprisingly easy, because in the nature of things the concerns of the Thompson family, which were all that they discussed among themselves apart from their immediate surroundings, could generate no real heat or feeling, seeing that they were non-existent. There were never, for instance, any awkward pauses between Caroline and her Mother, because the rules limited their possibilities of contact to the unemotive subjects of their lessons, and silences didn't have to be broken, either for themselves or for appearances: for themselves, they were the welcome silences of temporary and refreshing departure from the stage; for others, they seemed to be the comfortable silences of long association.

A routine was established as invariable as the routine of the flat. Angela breakfasted alone in her room. At about ten o'clock Mother, equipped for the *plage*, knocked at her door, and they crossed the road together and went down the steps to the piece of private beach that Mother had unhesitatingly selected the first morning— perhaps this also had been arranged. They had a mattress each, and there was a large umbrella, a wooden table, and two deckchairs. Mother, who spoke fluent French with a Belgian accent (Mrs Thompson had been to school in Brussels and there was an obscure Belgian connexion), insisted always that their colony should be at the very edge of the almost stationary sea. She secured it each day, as well as instant response when she looked round for the *garçon*. One thing Angela learned about Mother which had not been in the lessons was that she always got what she wanted.

Angela followed Mother's lead without question, except that she went regularly into the sea (after the first day Mother merely paddled once a morning in the shallows). Mother suggested mildly that Angela should not swim too far out and Angela accepted this as a warning of danger from human agency rather than from the tideless Mediterranean, and was careful to obey her. Both women read and dozed and dreamed on the sands, and hardly spoke to one another. It was extraordinarily undemanding and comfortable. Angela thought she could understand the success of arranged marriages.

Much later in the morning Father and Peter joined them, and eventually all four retired from the sun, under the wattle roofing of the restaurant at the back of the beach, and had drinks and a salad lunch.

Of course there was a fresh disappointment in not having Gerald with her on the beach, and there was another after lunch, when she was sent to her room. She didn't want to go, she yearned for the one thing she was never allowed to have, solitary exploration (or better still, exploration with Gerald), but go she must, and lock the outer door as she did at night, but not the door which connected with the room on her left. This room was occupied by Gerald, and they had told her to leave it unlocked.

'Then if you have a bad dream,' said Gerald, smiling, 'and call out, I can come and wake you up.'

It was a great comfort to know that Gerald was on the other side of the wall, always within reach. At first Angela was hopeful that he might make use of the door without an emergency and establish a toing and froing between them, but she was disappointed again. When he saw her to her room he said goodbye to her at her outside door, pecked her cheek if it was bedtime, but always left her there, not to be seen again until the beach, or the Croisette in the early evening, or the hotel terrace before dinner. Angela consoled herself by supposing that like her he had been given his instructions.

Mother came for her again in the late afternoon, half-past four to five o'clock, and they went down to the Croisette and squeezed into the busy pavement overflow of a café and drank tea and, if lunch had sufficiently dispersed, ate *tartes aux fraises* or *cafés liègeois*, watching the continuous parade. Then they strolled down a side street to the rue d'Antibes and along beside the shop windows. Mother might go in and buy small things—a box of crystallised fruits, a pretty handkerchief—and very frequently Angela would exclaim over this or that which caught her eye. Mother would respond invariably with a 'Yes, dear, it's very nice', or a 'No, it isn't very attractive, is it?', but she never expressed a taste, so that Angela, revealing so much of her own likes and dislikes, got to know no more of her Mother's tastes than she knew of her temperament.

When they had gone quite a long way along the rue d'Antibes they would turn back to the Croisette, look in some of the small galleries and boutiques (Mother did exclaim about the prices), then cross the road and sit down on deck-chairs, at that point just before the paths among the trees give place to the single wide pavement that lines the centre of the bay.

Here, eventually, Father and Peter would find them, and all four of them would sit on, in the freshening air, watching the constant stream of ordinary and extraordinary people, and amusing themselves (genuinely, it seemed to Angela) by making comments.

There was plenty to comment on. Men hand in hand; an elderly woman, every muscle straining in her face, looking up beseechingly at a young lover—or perhaps an overly-possessed son; frail, elegant, elderly widows; girls with round globes of bottoms in the tightest of jeans—emerald, scarlet, *le tartan;* happy families with children ranging in age from teenagers to babies; clever people in clever clothes, impressing each other as they went along; the occasional witless wanderer, stopping to address the air or a face which appeared in the way of the distance into which he was staring. If anyone was hurried, or unduly purposeful, they stood out like a sudden gust at the heart of a breeze. Angela knew why almost everyone in Cannes walked at the same leisurely pace: it was because this was the rhythm of the place. She, who even in the safe days before the ball used to charge along pavements with her head down, now found herself on every occasion—daylight or dark—maintaining this gentle articulated movement of the legs.

Sometimes Caroline and Peter became somewhat sharp in their comments on the eccentricities of passers-by, and then Mother would reprimand them vaguely (as if her mind was really somewhere else), and Father would try and make them feel ashamed of themselves. Angela thought this was the time of day she most enjoyed, as heat and colour slowly ebbed from the world around them and the prospect of dinner came up on the horizon. But she had to admit that the whole process of being a pebble on the beach selected by M was highly agreeable, even when devoid of that romance which she had originally imagined would be its principal ingredient. Now, however, she found that she didn't miss romance, she was content with Gerald's companionship and the development of a dialogue between them on a variety of impersonal topics which she could only believe that he relished as much as she did. Also none of them, of course, was ever completely relaxed. Angela suspected that it was the continuing possibility of danger in the midst of their seemingly tranquil existence that gave the spice to life which she might otherwise have looked for in a romance.

Dark comes down quickly on the Mediterranean coast. When they strolled back to the hotel in the evening it was still daylight—at least, it wasn't dark or even dusk, although the light held that weird weak intensity that heralds its departure. By the time they had separated on the landing, and Angela had crossed her room and gone out on to her tiny balcony where there was just space to stand and lean, as on a ship's rail, the sky was brilliant dark blue, lights threaded the foot of the Esterels opposite, arcs of light streamed away each side of her around the curves of the bay, and to the west Le Suquet seemed to smoulder in the deep amber light which, hardly illuminating it, yet threw up its every facet.

The sun's rim dips, the stars rush out,
At one stride comes the dark . . .

Angela had said this, softly but aloud, on each of the three evenings she had stood on her balcony before dinner. The world was so achingly lovely, it was hard, each time, to return to the room. But it was fun to dress up in the pretty Caroline frocks and join the family on the terrace in front of the hotel, above and beside the Croisette, where Caroline's and Peter's comments on the passers-by were pointed slightly by their drinks. They had dined, so far, in the hotel. Angela had been on tenterhooks, the first evening, wondering how completely the routine of the flat was to be disrupted, and had found it difficult to suppress a protest when she was packed off to bed immediately they rose from the table.

But she had been very tired, and the next night bed wasn't mentioned until they had spent a post-prandial hour strolling again along the Croisette and sitting down at a crowded pavement café for final drinks.

It was all delightful . . .

Angela, with the minimum of movement, raised the stand under the top half of her mattress, then lay back comfortably against it, staring at the sea. Mother slept on. A man approached over the sand, carrying a sack of English newspapers. It occurred to Angela that she had seen no newspaper, nor heard any news, since Gypsy's crumpled *Daily Mirror*. They had given her a little money, and she hailed the man (at least she didn't have to pretend that her French was better or worse than it was) and bought a paper. The biggest headline said 'Savage Storms in the South'. The international crisis which had been boiling on the front page when Angela disappeared was now simmering on the second. There didn't, today, appear to be anything to take its place beyond the outsize weather report. Angela wondered if there could be any news paragraph which might have a bearing on the fact that she was sitting on a French beach, and she began systematically to search each page.

'You look purposeful,' said a pleasant male voice.

Angela arrested her violently agitated response, hoping that her over-reaction had gone unnoticed. Oh, there had been no trials, as yet.

A young man had crouched down on the sand beside her and was smiling at her, a young man with wide-spaced green eyes, straight floppy brown hair and an anxious-to-please face. Angela called it a 'silly ass' face in her mind, but liked it.

'Oh, not really,' said Caroline. 'It's just that I've been such a complete ostrich since I got here that I thought I'd do a blitz on the paper and then put my head back in the sand.' She dropped the paper, feeling absurdly that it was somehow in-criminating. 'Not that there seems to be much.'

'There never is, really. At least, it always keeps.' He held something out to her. 'Forgive my disturbing you, by the way. I rescued this for you.' Angela looked harder at the object he held in his hand, and saw that it was one of her sandals, plastered with wet sand. She looked at him in surprise and he laughed: a gentle moderate laugh, noted Angela somewhere. 'I fished it out of the sea,' he said. 'I was—looking at you'—for the first time the almost naïve gaze flickered aside—'and I saw that evil mongrel pounce on it beside your feet and cart it off. Then it was just a simple pursuit into the shallows and—here you are.'

He put the sandal back beside its fellow. Angela glanced at Mother but she was still asleep. She said 'Thanks awfully' and waved a vague hand and the young man took the strain off his thighs and perched on the edge of her towel. She smiled at him, not knowing whether she wanted him to go or stay . . .

The sun was getting very hot, and the young man's shins were scarlet. Angela leaned over, unscrewed the top of her sun lotion, and held it out to him.

'I think you could do with some of this,' said Angela, and the evil mongrel whipped by again and knocked her hand, so that the young man received a cascade of sun lotion down his afflicted legs. They both laughed. He certainly had a nice laugh, although Angela was apprehensive that the ice was broken. Well, her lessons during those five days had been geared to just this moment.

'I'm Alan Boyce.'

'Caroline Thompson.' She smiled briefly at him again, turned and looked out to sea.

Mother awoke with a noticeable jerk.

'Good heavens, Caroline, what time is it?'

Caroline started to fish in her bag for her watch, but Alan Boyce said:

'Just gone noon.' He had nice hands.

'Father and Peter should be here any time now,' said Angela. 'Oh, Mother, this is Alan Boyce. My mother.'

Alan mumbled and Mother said 'How are you?', crisply cordial, switching immediately back to Angela. 'No,' said Mother, 'I forgot to tell you that I said we'd meet them in the hotel bar today. I thought I'd have had enough sun by twelve noon—and I have.'

There was still no sign of it.

'We'd better go, then.' Angela wasn't really sorry. If she postponed question time often enough, it might never arrive.

Mother said: 'Excuse us, Mr . . . er . . .'

'Boyce. Alan Boyce.'

Angela avoided his eye while she gathered her things together. When she got to her feet she made a vague gesture at the sun equipment. 'Be our guest.'

'You're not coming back, then?' There

was, perhaps, disappointment in the voice, although the smile was unvarying.

'Not today,' said Mother. Angela admired the way in which she avoided revealing any part of the routine.

'Thanks, then I will.'

Alan Boyce sat down in one of the deck-chairs. Angela and Mother said good-bye and moved away. At the top of the stairs they met Father and Peter and Mother said, quickly:

'I'm sorry, I knew I'd forget. We said we'd meet you in the hotel bar this morning. In the cool. I had too much sun yesterday. I think we both did.'

'We forgot too, all of us forgot,' said Gerald. They juggled for a moment at the top of the stairs, because the men tried to let the women go first yet were standing above them, and Angela had difficulty in controlling a hysterical giggle, it convulsed her still as they crossed the road back to the hotel, although she managed to hide it. She was beginning to get good at doing this, because she was having to exercise control over obstreperous giggles more and more frequently.

Father and Gerald turned towards the cool dark bar, and Mother said:

'We'll go upstairs first. Order me a campari and soda.'

'Caroline?' asked Father.

There was no real choice. At lunch time she had a soft drink, in the evening a vermouth or martini (plain) and a glass of wine at table. This was evidently considered suitable for Angela, at least while she had to sustain a part in a play, and Caroline had had a recent slight liver upset.

'*Citron pressé*, please,' said Angela, and she and Mother walked the wide, shallow arc of stair to their rooms on the first floor. They parted on the landing in their usual silence, but as Angela dumped her beach bag on her bed she noticed that a scarf of Mother's was caught in the top of it. On an impulse, stopping only to run a comb quickly through her hair and knock the worst of the sand from between her toes, Angela seized her handbag and the scarf and sped along the landing. She knocked on her Mother's door, curious to see if there would be any note of strain in the response.

But the soft, high, rather breathless voice called out, uninterested:

'*Qui est là?*'

'It's Caroline. Can I come in?' As she spoke Angela gently tried the handle but it didn't yield. She had to wait a moment until the catch was released and the door opened. Mother stood in the doorway, looking at her coldly.

'May I come in a minute, please, Mother?' asked Angela. She heard a note of reproof in her voice as she spoke, and perhaps Mother heard it too, because she made a submissive gesture and stood to one side, her arms hanging loosely as if to emphasise that she was offering no physical objection. Angela went into the room, and Mother followed and locked the door.

'Well?' she asked, with slight impatience. She sat down at the dressing-table and studied her face in the glass. Except for the considerable array of bottles on the glass top, the room looked untenanted. But Mother's scent had claimed every corner of it.

Mother picked up a comb and began to prink the ends of her hair.

'Nothing, really,' said Angela, perching on the arm of a chair and feeling increasingly awkward, 'I just found your scarf on top of my basket.' She laid it on the dressing-table, and Mother nodded. There was a silence. Angela had received sufficient warning to have no intention of playing it any way but in character. It was an extraordinary situation, all the same, the sustained myth through which, or not at all, things must be found out or conveyed. Exciting, though.

'I don't think you liked that young man much, did you, Mother?' she observed.

'I've nothing against him.' Mother noticed something on her face, and dropped the comb to pick up a tissue. She began busily to wield it. 'I'm not all that keen on people who force an introduction, but I shouldn't think there's any harm in him.' Her eyes had been flickering about, but with great effect she suddenly focused them, and looked hard into Angela's eyes through the mirror.

'I agree with you, but actually, he did have a reason,' said Angela, 'he rescued my shoe from the sea.'

'He'd been watching you,' said Mother.

'Perhaps.' Angela felt a stab of fear. Mother was fastening a chain round her neck, her head down. 'I don't think I'll encourage him.' Part of her was thinking, what a pity not to be able to take straightforward pleasure in this, there have been so few people to encourage. Caroline said, with a laugh: 'Anyway, we don't know where he's been!'

It was as near to the question as she could get.

'You're probably wise,' said Mother. Her eyes probed Angela's again, for a brief moment the fussy movements to her face and hair ceased. 'Anyway,' said Mother, eyes darting aside, head turning and hands busy, 'you've got a dancing partner and you're fond of your brother.'

There was no expression in her voice or her face. Angela felt puzzled.

'Yes, of course. Of course I am.'

Mother snapped a drawer shut. 'And Fred and Joe are coming. Did you remember that?'

Fred and Joe were a couple with a little building business in Petersham. They did things for the Thompsons—painting jobs, repointing the outside of the house, recently adding a small extension. By an amusing coincidence they had booked in at the same hotel for their holidays.

'Oh, I remembered.'

Angela got up and went over to the window. The shore was locked in heat, Le Suquet a sketch in black and white.

'This is a super place,' she said, 'I'm glad we've come here. I'm enjoying myself.' She tried to keep her sense of surprise out of her voice. Caroline would certainly have expected to enjoy herself.

'Are you? That's good.' The voice sounded so defeated and listless that Angela spun round. Mother had slumped on the dressing-stool and was staring with wide unseeing eyes into the mirror. She looked small and vulnerable and unhappy. Angela, unthinking, was across the room, standing behind Mother and putting her hands on Mother's shoulders. Mother had begun to pull herself together before Angela touched her, but when she met Angela's concerned eyes in the mirror she flopped again, sighed, smiled slightly, and said:

'You're a good kind girl.'

'Nonsense.' Angela squeezed the shoulders, in her pleasure at being given a reason to feel slightly warm towards her mother. 'I just didn't like to see you looking so woebegone.'

Mother laughed. Angela thought it was the first time she had laughed spontaneously since they had met.

'I've no special right, dear. Things have been hard for you, and you keep . . .'

The lapse was endearing, even though Mother immediately shook her head and looked angry. Angela said, turning away after a final squeeze of the shoulders:

'Shall we go down to Father and Peter? And I'm getting hungry.'

'Yes, dear.'

Things were improved between them. Mother picked up the brush again, but this time made more constructive movements with it. 'By the way, Caroline, we're dining at Palm Beach tonight. *Tenue de soirée. Attractions'*—(she pronounced it the French way, in inverted commas)—'Very gay and gala. You must make yourself look beautiful.'

'Huh,' said Angela, but interested, and running in quick mental review through Caroline's grander dresses. A snatch of accordion music came winding through the window like a wisp of chiffon. Angela went across the room again and looked out. On the Croisette a man was taking a photograph of an elderly woman, posed beside a sleepy-looking leopard held on a chain. A small group was talking animatedly round a bicycle with a buckled front wheel and a youth mopping his knee. Alan Boyce was just crossing the road from the beach, his hands in his pockets, his face amiably expressionless. The snatch of music was repeated.

Angela had a moment of exhilaration, of confidence, of nameless excitement to come.

In the doorway Mother stood still for a moment, looking perplexed. Then she patted Angela's hand with an abrupt gesture and said, her back to Angela as she locked the door:

'Nothing personal dear, *of course*, but

I'd rather you didn't come to my room another time.'

CHAPTER 7

The wide corridor of the Palm Beach casino was lined with mirrors and flowers. Dance music could be heard from a distance. Mother and Caroline left their wraps. Caroline's dress was a sleeveless green tunic, flaring to a chiffon swirl. Mother's chiffon was controlled, all cyclamen tucks and ruches. As they walked towards the music, Angela caught sight of a tall female walking to meet them, a taller male figure at its side. She thought, with a pang:

'Now, *that's* what . . .' and stopped. Gerald stopped too, laughing at her astonished face.

'Yes, it's only brother and sister. What do you think of us?'

'I—I envied us!'

She grinned at him, squeezed his hand. He looked magnificent in his white jacket, a few discreet frills on his shirt, his thick hair shining under the chandeliers. And she had had no pimples to doctor this

132

evening, no lank mousy hair to try and animate. Her sunburned face was framed in softly waving fair hair, her eyes were no longer wary, they shone with confidence and excitement. She had noticed them in the mirror when she was getting ready, and they had looked back at her boldly, like another woman's eyes.

Well, that was right, they were Caroline's, and the figure floating along the wide corridor of the Palm Beach casino was Caroline. It wasn't surprising that she was more sophisticated than Angela, because she was three years older. Admittedly she didn't use her head so much—she didn't give Angela's Oxford Entrance work a thought—but she was far more at ease . . .

The huge room was full of music and murmur and changing lights. The Thompsons were given a table against the wall, which Angela thought was something of an achievement when there were barely three available walls and a great mass of tables in the centre of the room, right up to the platform where the orchestra was playing and round the small dance floor. But it was probably prudent, as well as more agreeable, for the Thompson family to have one direction from which nothing unexpected could come.

Peter had told Mother and Caroline when they left the hotel that they were looking exceptionally elegant, but now Angela saw that expensive elegance was the norm. She thought she had never seen such costly and successful painstaking, such gowns, such hair styles, such jewels, such seeming beauty, gathered in one place.

Yet the atmosphere—of old and young together, of the unbreached conventions of dress and dancing—reminded Angela of the Bella Ball.

She said to Gerald when they were dancing—they danced right away, leaving their dinner choices with Mother and Father to transmit to the waiter—

'This makes me think of that ball we went to the other day at home. With the parents. This is a hundred times more elegant and sophisticated, of course, but it's the same idea, really.'

'Yes?'

It was as if he settled comfortably back, to see what she was up to.

Angela hesitated for a moment, then reminded herself that she was dancing with her brother.

'I never tackled you about that, did I? I must be slipping.'

She grinned at him, provocatively, and thought his hand tightened for a moment on her spine. But he said, resignedly:

'Out with it!'

'You seemed to be having rather a good time, Peter, with . . . oh, I can't remember her name—that tall girl with the long black hair and big mouth. Anyway, you should remember—every time there was a gap in the crowd there you were, wreathed round each other.'

That she was revealing the fact that Angela had seen, and had smarted, now seemed totally unimportant, the situation was so far away, so incapable of repetition (in effect, if not in fact). And it was exhilaratingly sweet to take her unique opportunity to mop up this small bloodletting—and to play verbal games that might draw pinpricks of blood from her brother adversary. It was exciting to have not the slightest idea what his reaction would be.

He exploded with laughter.

'Oh, sis! Were we? Were we really? I seem to remember thinking that she was an accommodating lassie. I can't remember her name either.'

'She does have a bit of a lurid reputation,' said Angela happily, enjoying her

135

belated revenge on the evermore defenceless Christine Bolam.

'Anyway, I took *you* home,' said Gerald. Angela said, 'Yes' gravely, looking at him, and then their eyes slid away from each other and he tightened his arm round her and danced with her in silence, his cheek just touching hers.

'But didn't you follow it up?' she must whisper, eventually.

'There was hardly time,' answered Gerald, and Angela began to laugh, and went on laughing and laughing, until Gerald said, suddenly sharp in her ear:

'Clever but not too clever. Confident but not over-confident!' and she pulled away from him and looked at his polite, smiling, inexpressive face, as chastened as she had been almost hysterical, and he pulled her to him again and they finished the dance in silence.

So she was in a more or less equable state when they sat down. A cinzano was waiting for her, the outside of the glass furred with cold. Father offered a toast to their holiday, which they drank with little smiles to each other over the rims of their glasses. Angela felt uncomplicatedly fond of all three of them, and was glad that Mother, too, offered a fleeting smile. Since their arrival Mother had looked excessively tight-lipped, with wandering eyes.

Angela put her hand out to touch Mother's where it lay on the table. Mother pulled her hand sharply away as if Angela had stung her, looked from Father to Gerald, blushed, and then laid her hand on Angela's where it had recoiled.

'Forgive me, dear, I was miles away.'

'You were dreaming of a serpent,' said Gerald, and Mother gave a nervous giggle.

'What ridiculous things you say, Peter!'

'Do I?'

Angela saw that he was grinning at Mother as if challenging her, but Mother merely shrugged her shoulders and touched the edges of her mouth with a tiny white handkerchief, releasing a wave of perfume which made Angela draw back.

'Will you dance with me Mother, please,' invited Gerald, his face now composed.

Mother moved quickly, then sank slowly back.

'Oh, Peter, I don't think . . .'

'Come on!'

He was on his feet, tipping her chair back, and she got up with what Angela suspected was mock reluctance. Angela watched them, for as long as she could until they were lost in the crowd. Mother looked so tiny beside Peter, putting her head back in order to see into his face, his head lowered towards her, both her hands on his shoulders, both his round her waist . . . Angela had a vision of Gerald and Christine Bolam, an old familiar vision, complete with memory of her own reaction as she had seen them, then remembered with a surge of triumph that the picture was defeated.

She took a gulp of her drink as she turned back to face Father. Father remained the one awkward family situation—because she had never been alone with him before, and their meetings in company hardly advanced her knowledge of him—although no doubt they supplemented his of her.

He was gazing with apparent benevolence at the throng of dancers. 'This is a nice evening, Father,' said Caroline gratefully. How strange to be thanking one's Father, and not having the least idea whether or not he was responsible for one's entertainment!

Father turned his mild gaze on to his daughter. He had very light, rather weak-looking eyes, which Angela was never sure were resting on her or not.

'I'm glad you're enjoying it. Later we'll go into the *salle de jeux*. Initiate you into a small strange world, now that you're twenty-one.'

Another small strange world, mentally corrected Angela. She felt a thrill of excitement. Even Caroline wasn't really blasé, and did things for the first time.

'Father, how marvellous. Will you be giving me some gambling money?'

'You may have sixty francs. When you've lost it you can watch the big spenders.'

'Sixty francs. That's fantastic!'

'One chip costs twenty, Caroline.'

'Never!'

'It does. So if you want to feel you're taking part—take your time.'

'Are you going to dance with me?'

'You know I only dance with your mother, and then only under protest.'

They smiled at each other. Even this was easy.

Angela drained her glass. The first course arrived, with another cinzano, and a few minutes later Mother and Peter, smiling at each other. Peter said, as he helped Mother into her chair:

'Mother, there is nobody, but nobody, like you,' and she leaned up and patted his cheek. Angela envied him his ease in his role. What fun Anouilh must have had, writing *Dinner with the Family!*

Although no fictional ingenuity could be as ingenious as the real, or the unreal, thing . . .

'Good evening!'

Angela, drifting off in the direction of her current metaphysical preoccupations, jumped, and focused her unseeing eyes into the nearby smiling face of Alan Boyce. Her first reaction was annoyance that he should materialise at this point, rather like an unwanted exam on a half holiday, and her second a sort of . . . what was it? Something she didn't approve of and would look at later—whatever it was, it was to do with her realisation that he was not alone, he had in tow a determined-looking young woman with a noticeably white skin and cloudy dark hair.

'This is Winifred Holland,' said Alan Boyce. 'Are you enjoying yourselves?'

'Of course,' said Angela brightly, nodding at Winifred Holland. The girl had large capable-looking hands, one of which was clasped in one of Alan's, and wore a rather unbecoming dark dress which hung awkward and Angela-like on her big shoulders. Caroline saw this, before Angela saw the clear intelligence in the wide-spaced eyes and high forehead. The girl's lips were drawn tightly together. Had there been a quarrel?

Alan was nodding cheerfully to Mother, who nodded graciously in return, and Angela said:

'Oh, forgive me, you haven't met all of us, have you? My father—my brother Peter. Alan Boyce.'

Murmured greetings were exchanged, followed by a pause. Alan Boyce seemed to be one of those people who are temperamentally incapable of taking leave even when all necessity for their continued presence has passed, while yet exhibiting an almost frantic anxiety to be off (indeed, the difficulty of departure tends to be in proportion to the strength of that anxiety).

'I'm afraid there really isn't room for one more chair at this table, let alone two,' said Mother at last, apologetically but firmly, and Alan started anguishedly to protest that he had no intention, that he was just toddling off, while Gerald asked,

'Are you on your own?'

'Yes, and quite self-sufficient!' said Winifred Holland, with suddenly a smile so charming that there was no snub in her words for the Thompsons, rather an admonition to a less than ardent admirer, and Alan's expostulations turned into a:

'By jove, yes, quite!'

and a quiet look of astonished admiration

at Winifred (similar, Angela thought, to the look he had given Caroline when she turned to face him on the beach). Winifred, with a deprecating smile, pulled him away.

Gerald looked quizzically at Angela.

'You didn't tell me, sis?'

'There wasn't anything to tell.'

Nevertheless Caroline had seen an ever-so-small shadow over her gaiety, if only for a moment. Angela didn't approve: she had never hunted scalps, and it was the reaction of the scalphunter which had checked Caroline when Winifred appeared.

'Who is he?' Father asked.

'Someone who started chatting with Caroline on the beach,' said Mother.

'He rescued my sandal from an evil mongrel. We don't know anything about him except his name.'

'We didn't get any further,' said Mother, 'because I remembered we had arranged to meet you in the hotel bar.'

'I see,' said Father.

'He seems to have fallen out more fruitfully this evening.' This from Gerald.

'He only returned me my sandal.'

One waiter arrived with the wine, another with the main course. Caroline, who shared with Angela a hearty appreciation of food, forgot about Alan Boyce. But when she was dancing with Gerald again, after a *tarte aux pêches*, a coffee, and a *crème de menthe*, she asked him if he was growing into a possessive brother.

'Only a protective one,' he murmured.

'That I like.'

The floor was even more crowded now, and her brother held her very close. She felt joyously light-hearted.

'Father tells me we're going gambling.'

'So he tells me.'

'You've done it before, of course.'

She knew that Peter had been quite often to France, but how little she knew about Gerald!

'A few times, yes.'

'What shall I play, Peter, as a novice?'

'Roulette, I should say. It combines outlay and excitement in the most suitable proportions.'

'At twenty francs a time?'

'*Trente et quarante* is slow. Evens only. The others—right out of your class.'

'I'll be guided.'

'It's something you're learning. You've got a crumb on your chin.' He removed it, gently.

'Is my nose shiny?'

'A bit. But it's a brown shine.'

'That's something I can't take your word for. You've awakened a tiny little anxiety about my appearance. And I want to go to the loo.'

'*Naturellement*. This minute?'

'Not this minute.'

They danced in silence. The music was tuneful and romantic, sometimes the accordion got the melody and she shivered with a vague sense of possibilities. Once in a gap she saw Alan and Winifred dancing together, Winifred kept at a distance and listening gravely as Alan held forth. Alan caught Angela's eye and nodded encouragingly.

'You've learned to accept silence,' said Gerald suddenly, into her ear.

'What on earth do you mean?'

'I mean—when you were—younger—you tended to be uneasy if you weren't always talking.'

'Even inside the family?'

She thought they were both surprised at her irony.

'Even—inside the family. At least, where a Special Occasion was involved, where you felt Certain Things were Due. Now—you let it happen.'

'That's a good thing, is it?'

'I should say, yes, it is.'

'Remember,' said Angela, laughing, 'I'm of mature years now, Peter, I'm twenty-one. I'm growing up.'

144

He took his cheek away from beside hers to look at her gravely. Again for an instant Angela saw that strange fleeting sadness.

'I think you are.'

Angela recalled her first dance with Gerald at the Bella Ball, when each minute of silence had seemed to her a minute of failure. How much he had noticed about her, looking over her head into the crowd, dancing amorously with Christine Bolam, never watching her face! Whatever happened—as long as they both lived—they would have some sort of a bond.

When she found herself standing in front of the pink-tinted mirrors in the ladies' cloakroom, elegant handbowls to each side of her, Angela was unable to escape more memories of the Bella Ball and the eager group of young women who had surrounded her. Fielding them, she had glanced up into the mirror and into her own suspicious eyes. She tried to repeat the gesture, but now it seemed impossible, she looked so different, her eyes persisted in being confident, her hair framed her face. Angela smiled at her reflection, bent forward to repair her lipstick . . .

'*Angela!*'

The lipstick swerved, marking a pink swathe from mouth to chin. Angela spun round, clutching at the basin to steady her fluttering heart. Two English girls had apparently rushed towards each other with cries of delighted recognition.

Winifred Holland came out of one of the loos and looked at her. With concern.

'Are you all right?'

'Yes, of course.' Angela made herself laugh. 'Why do you ask?'

'You've smudged your lipstick and your eyes are enormous, as if you'd seen a ghost—and you had your hand on your heart!'

'I have seen a ghost—in the mirror,' said Angela hectically. 'Why does one always look so absolutely awful in ladies' cloakroom mirrors? Everybody else always looks cool and elegant, but oneself . . . Ah, well . . .' She turned back to the mirror, savagely swallowing her heart down into her breast. She hated what she had just said, it was like fishing—and Caroline, amazingly, looked more attractive in the glass than Winifred. 'The sun helps a bit, I suppose. You haven't been here long, have you?'

Winifred smiled. 'It looks like that, doesn't it?'

'Oh, I'm sorry.' But any crudity was better than an admission of a *crise de nerfs*.

'I've been here for more than a week,'

said Winifred. 'The sun never does anything to my lily-white skin. Well, at least I don't go red.'

'Take care, all the same,' said Caroline mechanically, busy with her thoughts. Winifred had been lucky to meet up with a rich, amiable young man. She didn't look the type who would do well on holiday, but you could never tell.

'Oh, Alan doesn't let me sun for too long,' said Winifred, and Angela regretted Caroline's unkind assumption. She noticed a ring on Winifred's left hand—an engagement ring. Winifred was still combing her hair.

'I'll see you around,' said Caroline.

Winifred's mouth stretched briefly in the mirror and Angela, her legs still trembling, went out into the sumptuous corridor where Gerald awaited her.

'I met that Winifred girl in there, Peter, I think she must be engaged to Alan Boyce.'

'I met Alan Boyce in my place. She is.'

Alan came out of the men's cloakroom, smiling his amiable smile, and took up his station outside the ladies'. They all nodded, Gerald took Angela's hand, and they walked away.

'Did you talk to him much?'

147

'I didn't talk to him at all. He talked to me. Told me he was staying with the girl's grandmother. She has a villa in Super Cannes.'

And was what she seemed to be. A family for all seasons.

A sudden depression enfolded Angela, threatening her happiness. She found she was envying Winifred Holland the reality of her situation. How crazy she was, to mourn the non-existence of a non-existent family! But the sensation could become crushing, letting in thoughts of her own uncomfortable reality, of Mummy and Daddy imprisoned at home without her. Real people, suffering, as men suffered when other men attacked them, leaving them with blood pouring out of their mouths . . .

'We'll need our passports for the *salle de jeux*,' said Peter.

Again her agony was postponed.

'Oh, Peter, I didn't know. I haven't got mine.'

'You haven't got it, goose. Father has it. Remember?'

'Yes, of course.' Father had taken charge of all the passports.

'Don't get upset when they give you the once over,' said Gerald, as they walked between the mirrors and the flowers towards the lobby of the *salle*.

'Who, for goodness' sake?'

'The gentlemen of the anteroom. Those who guard the approaches to the *salle de jeux*. Legend has it that they never forget a face—and that they know a dishonest one when they see it.'

'We'll be all right, then.'

Gerald shot her what she thought might be an admiring glance. The marshalling process had begun again, marked by the now familiar tingle of excitement and apprehension. Long-term fears withdrew, once more, before the challenge of the moment.

'So—will they recognise you here, Peter?'

He glanced at her again. 'No. Not here.'

Mother and Father were at the counter. The four passports were spread out between them and a man on the far side. A neat dark man in a blue jacket, looking like the two other neat dark men who stood waiting at other points.

'*Voici les enfants!*' said Mother and Caroline said, nudging Peter, 'Well, *really!*'

The man raised his eyes from the passports, and looked gravely first at Gerald, then at Angela. It was funny, but she found it easier to hold his eye and look gravely back at him than it had been at the Customs barrier last summer, when she had been what she seemed, with a blameless suitcase.

Still without expression, the man copied various particulars out of the passports, made out a chit for each of them, returned the passports.

'*Huit jours, monsieur?*'

'*Huit jours,*' confirmed Father.

So they would be in Cannes another week. Or perhaps they wouldn't. Not that it mattered. Angela had almost ceased to look for clues, she had almost begun to prefer the open-ended situation where there was no discernible future. It seemed, in the circumstances, the less fraught of alternatives.

'*Amusez-vous bien!*' said the man behind the counter, catching Caroline's eye, and smiling. It was an unexpected reaction, but Angela reflected that he must, after all, smile sometimes at his wife, or his children. She inclined her head gravely, as befitting one who was of age to enter *salles de jeux*, and followed Mother and Father through the double doors.

The room was large, with a high elaborate ceiling, so that the people beneath it seemed small and, appropriately in such a place, insignificant, as in those Boudin coast scapes, where they stagger ashore from Channel paquebots, in the bottom inch of the picture, under huge unkindly skies.

Not that the people in the *salle de jeux* at Palm Beach had any appearance of disarray. On the contrary. Angela was struck by the quietness and orderliness of what was quite a large crowd. As in the dinner dance, the women seemed without exception to be elegant and beautifully dressed, with a preponderance, now, of watchful, inscrutable faces and expensively ringed hands. The people were crowded impassively round the tables, leaving great promenade spaces where nobody walked, and at the bar Angela saw only one or two individuals perched, she thought moodily, on stools. Against the wall of glass at the far side of the room were a few armchairs, vacant except for one occupied by a stout red-faced woman trying to repair her make-up. To the right, slightly raised and roped off, was the restaurant, its tables continuing through on to the open terrace, the only area which escaped the pervading sense of dedication. The atmosphere of the *salle de jeux*, in fact, in the first moment that she entered it, reminded Angela of the atmosphere of a church.

'Peter will take care of you, Caroline,' said Mother, not looking at Angela but gazing eagerly across the room with face faintly flushed. Father had already left them and was carrying out a transaction at one of the little windows in the wall.

'What are you going to play, Mother?' asked Gerald. Angela wondered why he looked amused.

'Roulette, of course!'

The flush deepened. Father came back with handfuls of chips—round, square, oblong—and gave three round ones to Angela.

'Thanks, Father.'

Father said to Gerald:

'You'll take care of yourself.' Gerald bowed.

Mother took hold of Father's arm and tried to pull him away but he looked at Angela and said:

'We shan't be staying long. It's late already.'

'Whenever you want to go,' said Gerald, and took Angela's hand, and led her off among the tables.

'You know,' said Angela, aware while she was talking of moving among brown faces and smooth brown shoulders and jewellery and expensive conflicting scents,

'I think Father was saying that to Mother then, really.'

He shot her a glance. 'What makes you think that?'

'Because Mother was all agog. She must be a gambler. She was pawing the ground like a horse at a starting gate. Didn't you notice?'

'Oh, yes, I noticed.'

'Then why be so surprised that I did? Men are so arrogant!'

'Sorry, sis.' He sounded repentant, but Angela thought he was trying not to laugh.

'I'll forgive you. Thousands wouldn't. Now instruct me.'

Gerald looked round.

'Four roulette tables along here. Two of them with fifty franc minimum stakes. Strictly for watching, those. This one'—he put his hands at her waist and manoeuvred her into a small space so that she was almost standing against a table—'is twenty francs. Best to lose your money here. I'm going to change some.'

'Shall I wait for you?'

'Not especially. I'll see you around.'

It was quite some time before Angela even started to think about using the three chips she held clasped in her hand. It was enough to watch the precision of the croupiers, the shuttered faces round the tables, and the busy hands; to discover the austere attraction of the red and black and green baize.

It was a game of small recurrent sounds: the croupiers' spare remarks; the requests of the players who couldn't reach—French, English, would-be French; the whirr of the pebble at speed inside the wheel, then its climactic dance down over the numbers until its selection of a slot and the final silent revolutions; the sound of the rake on tight-drawn cloth and the clink of lost chips, then of the winning ones as they were adroitly selected, piled up by the croupier and pushed by rake across the table.

Angela watched the complete process half a dozen times before separating one of her three chips and looking at it. Twenty francs it said, in the centre, and she hesitated, thinking of what twenty francs would do in the way of *cafés liègeois* and newspapers. Angela decided she would, in fact, be just as well amused if she went on watching other people winning and losing and changed the chips into money. But Caroline was anxious to have a bet, and realised that if she placed a chip on the conjunction of the numbers 17,18, 20 and 21 she would cover the ages of herself and Angela, which seemed as good an offering to chance as any other. And if she won, she would get eight or nine more twenty franc pieces.

'*Dix-sept, vingt-et-un, s'il vous plaît,*' said Caroline to the croupier, who took the chip and placed it without looking because he was looking at Caroline with an unconcealed interest, which Angela would have considered rude if it hadn't been so entirely unself-conscious.

As it was, Caroline was not displeased. She leaned away from the table, smiling to herself, stumbled, and realised that her feet were not quite touching the floor. Also, people and things had acquired a slight blur to their edges. She was, in fact, not quite sober. Well, she had drunk more than she had ever drunk before, and her current cheerful vague mood was quite new to her. In such a mood fate could only reward her.

But the little white ball jumped into the slot marked '36', and Caroline's stake was swept away with most of the rest. The disappointment, for a moment, was shockingly acute, and Angela turned away, trying to focus into the middle distance. She saw that Gerald was coming towards her, and as she stepped uncertainly forward to meet him, other people moved instantly into the space she had left.

'You've lost your place.' He looked down at her smiling, a few chips in his hand. 'You look cheerful. You've been winning!'

She shook her head, not trusting herself to speak because she would laugh, and there was really no call for it.

'You've lost it all!'

She shook her head again, then managed to say:

'Only one.'

'You're being very restrained.'

'It's so interesting just to *look*. Have you done anything yet?' The world was steadying.

'No. Like you I enjoy looking. For instance at that fifty franc table.' He waved an arm behind him. 'There's a little chap there who must be a millionaire several times over. Winning and losing a fortune at each throw. You can feel the atmosphere. You always can when there's really big money about. Come and have a look.'

He walked across with her. The fifty franc table was deep in people. Again, Gerald's hands went round her waist, manoeuvred her into a gap.

'Which man?' she whispered.

Gerald nodded across the table and, blinking and concentrating, she followed his glance to a pile of assorted chips and behind them a small man of indeterminate age and nationality with curly hair and a snub nose wearing an open-necked blue shirt which showed a lot of brown chest and a St Christopher medallion. The man's hands were rough and his nails not particularly clean.

'In the blue shirt?' Her breath caught and she hiccuped, but Gerald didn't appear to notice.

'Yes. You watch. I'm going to play a bit. Not here!'

He squeezed her waist and left her, and she turned eagerly back to the table, reflecting muzzily on the extraordinary fact that Gerald the beautiful, the unattainable, the symbol of the world from which her Angealness had once debarred her, had squeezed her waist and moved away, and she had let him go with no more sensation than relief that she could now quietly recover her equilibrium and enjoy the drama of the table. She no longer despised Caroline.

'*Rien ne va plus!*'

Nevertheless the curly-haired man in the blue shirt put an enormous oblong plaque on to the table. The croupier showed no reaction. The white pebble was losing speed. It clattered downwards, settled, moved round silently with the wheel.

'*Quatre. Rouge, pair et manque!*'

It was a good turn up for the bank. The rake came out, removed most of what was set out on the cloth, including the enormous plaque of the curly-haired man. Angela looked as hard into his face as her condition allowed, but it continued impassive, wearing an air of quiet good humour.

'*Messieurs, dames, faites vos jeux!*'

The man in the open-necked blue shirt this time placed two enormous plaques on the board and a sound like a sigh ran round the table. Angela could feel a rising tension.

'*Rien ne va plus!*'

No one spoke or moved, except to crane heads towards the wheel. Angela's view of it was now obscured by the gathering crowd, and she watched the faces. How many meagre old ladies there were, dressed like girls, their eyelids drooping, their faces intent, the flesh hanging on their thin arms in little tubes. She looked towards the man with curly hair and was surprised to see him get slowly to his feet and stroll over to another table. As the ball clattered into place she could see the back of his head.

'*Vingt-neuf. Noir, impair, passe!*'

The little man came slowly back to the table. No one had taken his chair and he sat down again, the people behind moving aside to ease his passage. The croupier pushed a large variegated heap of chips towards him, piled on two of the big oblongs. His expression was the same. He took the top four chips off the pile and tossed them to the croupier.

'*Merci, monsieur, les employés!*'

She was feeling a bit sick and would have to look for some fresh air.

She wavered to the doors, searching vaguely and unsuccessfully for any members of her family, smiling expansively at the blue-coated watchdogs outside. In the corridor she had to walk rather carefully in order to keep a straight course. She was glad to reach the ladies' cloakroom, and she went into one of the loos and locked the door and sat down. She closed her eyes but then she began to move in increasingly swift circles until something picked her up and hurled her against the door, and she hastily opened them again. She thought that after all there would be more air in the main room.

She looked pale in the pink-tinted mirrors, her eyes large and dark. She saw through the mirror that someone was standing very close behind her, looking at her in the glass in a puzzled hesitant way. Angela stared back in disbelief. It was Barbara Shaw, a girl in her form at school she wasn't particularly friendly with but had known for years. She saw herself broadly smiling.

'Barbara!'

The hesitation in the face behind her gave way to delighted recognition, and at the same instant Angela realised what she had done.

The awful thing was, she had had a chance, Barbara hadn't been at all sure, she was already half persuaded that she was looking at a stranger who resembled Angela Canford. All Angela would have had to do for Barbara to turn away was to stare back coldly through the glass. But she had made sure that Barbara had recognised her, and there was no going back on that.

It was, perhaps, the worst moment of her life . . .

'. . . You never let on you were going to France as early as this, Angela. You look great, by the way . . . Are you with your parents?'

Her lips were terribly stiff, in the mirror she thought her face looked dramatically ill.

160

'No,' she muttered, 'with friends. It was unexpected . . .'

'And with me, Angela!'

Dear God, don't let Mother come in, whatever else You do, don't let that happen!

She ought to say something, now she had revealed herself as Angela, she ought at least to behave normally, not give Barbara anything to think about when she left.

Dear God, please let her leave . . .

Barbara was doing enough talking for them both, at least. She was burbling on and on about how much she liked Cannes. Angela wished she could faint. She felt so peculiar that she might faint. But that would be the worst thing of all, like screaming 'Look at me!' . . .

What was Barbara saying?

'I'm terribly sorry, Angela, but I must fly, the parents are waiting by the door.'

'How long—are you here for?'

Barbara wrinkled her nose in displeasure.

'Tomorrow morning. It's all over. What rotten luck I didn't run into you sooner! See you in September, anyway. Have a good time, you lucky thing! 'Bye!'

In a whirl of gauzy stole and *muguet des bois* she had gone. Angela went back into

161

the loo and sat down to recover. Self-hate and thankfulness mingled in equal proportions. She would have liked to stay hidden for a long time, to stop trembling and to let Barbara and her parents get far away, but if she didn't go back the family would be worried about her.

When she came out of the loo the cloakroom was deserted. Angela thought she looked thinner and sharper in the face than she had looked after dinner, and she was surprised that her hair hadn't turned white. She peered fearfully into the corridor but there was no sign of Barbara, or of any anxious-looking Thompsons. But even as she craned towards the main doors, hands encircled her waist and she spun round.

'Good Lord, sis, have you seen a ghost?'

Winifred Holland had asked her the same question, in that other world which had been safe compared with this. Angela, the schoolgirl of eighteen, wanted to fling herself on Gerald's chest and blurt out her horrible indiscretion. And perhaps, already, there were only Angela left, and Gerald, and two other stateless persons. Perhaps she ought to tell Gerald, anyway, in case contingency plans were now necessary. But she couldn't.

'I don't think so.' She had to force herself to smile, as if it was a process she was only just learning. She put an arm through his as they walked back to the *salle de jeux*. She was so tense the arm was like a steel bar, and as he turned for a moment to look at her curiously, she tried consciously to relax.

'That man, Peter,' she said, as they rejoined the decorous crowd, 'the unlikely millionaire, he lost a fortune then won one. And didn't turn a hair either time.'

Her old trooper ability against odds was working again.

'Didn't I tell you? How's your money going?'

'I haven't used any more.'

'There's restraint for you.' He looked at her closely and she forced herself to return his gaze. 'You know, you don't look so good. Come and have a drink.'

'Thanks, Peter.' She was so clear-headed, so sober, it would be like her first.

She took his arm again. She felt vulnerable out of the crowd, sitting beside unsuspecting Gerald on a stool, with no one to either side of them. But the brandy warmed her chest and calmed the beating of her heart.

'Better?'

163

'Yes, thanks.'

She must not think of it. What she had done, she had done, and she would know soon enough if it was serious. Oh, God, how she hated herself. It was the most wretched sensation in the world, to hate and despise yourself, because you were stuck with it, you couldn't walk away.

Mother and Father came up, and Angela took another agonised and penitential swig of brandy.

'How goes it?' asked Gerald.

'Quite well.' Mother was her usual sallow self, but clutching a large number of chips and smiling more spontaneously than she usually did. Father shrugged.

'Me, I'd just as soon watch.'

'So would I,' said Angela. She held up her two chips.

'You look tired, Caroline,' said Father. 'Do you want me to change them for you?'

Angela nodded and slipped them into his hand. He turned to Mother.

'Will you have a drink?'

Oh, no, don't have a drink, say you're too tired, let's get away!

But Mother said yes, she thought she would like a brandy, Caroline had given her the idea, and they sat there for another half hour.

Father took Mother's chips out of her half-resistant hands and went off to change them. He insisted on Angela taking the cash equivalent of her two, and his kindness was another unendurable pang.

Walking again between the mirrors in the ante-rooms of Palm Beach, Angela would never have mistaken the figure she now saw reflected. Gerald told her she looked tired. Every second she was braced to hear Barbara's breathy ecstatic voice, but the family Thompson got back to the hotel without incident.

Outside her room Gerald searched her face, and she had, once again, to force down the impulse to blurt out to him the unbelievable thing she had done.

All night she fled Barbara—along streets, up and down stairs, through ornate lofty rooms. Only in the early morning, lying exhausted but at last free of nightmare, a cautious optimism crept in with the first sunlight, and Caroline told Angela to stop being such a fusspot.

165

CHAPTER 8

'I say, do you mind if I join you?'

The request was repeated, word for word, and with the same polite diffidence. The second time Angela realised she had heard it before, and lifted her head out of her hands. Alan Boyce was poised beside the neighbouring bar stool, a hand on the seat, a foot on the crossbar, awaiting a sign from her. He was alone. Angela waved her hand vaguely, and took a mouthful of coffee. Alan climbed up beside her.

Angela too was alone. After her breakfast she had decided, from a combination of headache and apprehension, to summon up courage to send Mother down to the beach without her. She had in fact remained in bed to give force to her decision.

But this morning, for the first time, Mother hadn't appeared, and as the minutes ticked away Angela had to realise that the routine had been interrupted.

Why had the routine been interrupted?

Angela thought of Barbara Shaw clattering down the steps of Palm Beach, calling to her parents through the clear air: 'I've just seen Angela Canford!' The words 'Angela Canford' would only, perhaps, have to hit the air to be taken up by the vigilants at the end of every sound wave, waiting attentive . . .

She lay for a horrible hour of speculation and mounting panic, until it reached a pitch where she had to leap out of bed and knock violently at the door which connected with Peter's room, shout his name. But there had been no response, and after that she had got dressed quickly and gone downstairs. It would be better to be taken in public than to wait in the dreadful concentration of privacy—and in public somebody might come to her aid.

No member of the family was to be seen. On the steps of the hotel the sun beamed on her with instant effect, out of a clear blue sky whose serenity was in no way disturbed by the possible disintegration of the family Thompson. It was a glorious morning. There were some tiny clouds on the low horizon, and the lightest of breezes, the Esterels and Le Suquet were wreathed in a fine-weather haze.

A few people dotted the terrace, mostly at its edges where trees mottled the sunlight. Nobody Angela knew, and she turned draggingly into the bar, where the dim cool seemed less painful a contrast to her fear.

The fear came in unheralded thrusts, like her headache. At its height it was unbearable, and she gripped the edge of the counter. Every voice was Barbara's, or those of the men whom she had alerted.

She ordered coffee. The barman looked at her with concern as he set it down.

'*Mademoiselle! Qu'est-ce qu'il y a? Peut-être avez-vous passé une soirée trop agréable?*' He began immediately to laugh at the idea, but Angela said:

'*C'est juste, Pierre, soyez gentil,*' and he looked at her again and turned away to polish glasses.

No such consideration from Alan Boyce, of course, whom Angela didn't imagine would be oversensitive to the sensitivities of others. On the other hand, he really was too bland to be an irritant, and she couldn't help liking him. She hoped she wouldn't involve him in any trouble.

'I say, you look a bit gloomy this morning.'

Angela managed a rueful smile.

'*Tout simplement:* I have a hangover.'

'No. Really?'

'Really. Oh, I didn't sing my way up to bed last night, or anything'—didn't she?—'but I obviously overdid it a bit. Mixtures, I suppose.'

'Try a prairie oyster.'

'Do you mind? Coffee will do the trick.'

'Think I'll have one too. All right?'

She waved her hand again and he wriggled into a more comfortable position and gave his order. Pierre obliged him instantly and he took the thick cup in both hands. His hands really were attractive—large but thin, with long fingers.

'I hope the rest of your family are in better shape.'

Oh, dear God, so did she!

'I haven't seen any of them yet. I rather think I'm the first down.'

Unless the others were lying somewhere other than their beds, blood pouring out of their mouths . . . Gypsy and Joe must have trained her well, she was still painting a portrait of a spoiled young woman. But Angela, too, had always been able to speak first, then worry second about what she was going to say.

'Where's Winifred?'

'On the beach. I felt I'd had enough sun for one session, and I came for a walk—and smelt the cool of this place.'

169

'You must have a very long nose.' She looked at it as he turned back to his coffee. It was straight and quite short, very slightly tip-tilted. She wondered if he had chosen this one of many cool bars because of Caroline. 'How are your shins?'

He pulled up a trouser leg. The flesh was slightly less angry. 'You see, your application did me good.'

Angela joined in the quiet laughter which was the second positively nice thing about Alan Boyce, after his hands. But in the middle of it she realised that it was almost twelve noon and the family still hadn't appeared—probably because she had destroyed it.

'I say, you aren't too good, are you?'

She shook her head, speechless.

'I'm surprised your brother's still in bed on a morning like this.'

'He doesn't usually . . .' Angela tailed off, realising that circumstances had been such, all along, that she had no idea of Gerald's habits in the mornings. She was now beginning to feel sick. To forget about it, she made a particular effort. 'Winifred told me you took care she didn't sit in the sun for too long.'

'So I do.' Alan drained his coffee cup. 'I have left her under an umbrella—or as the French more optimistically say, a parasol—with a towel over her legs. She has promised me to remain that way, unless she fancies a swim, in which case she is permitted fifteen minutes' fully exposed drying time.' He beamed at her cheerfully. 'I must say'—there was that sudden flash of humble admiration—'you're a very good colour.'

'Thank you.' Angela wondered how a man like Alan Boyce had ever come to the point of proposing marriage to one young woman, rather than another. But perhaps the main mover had been Winifred Holland—Angela had sensed determination. It was extraordinary how determined a woman could be over an indeterminate man . . .

A bar of sunlight lay across Alan's hand where it rested on the counter. Sipping at her coffee, watching the bar of sunlight come and go on Alan's hand with the movements of a breeze-stirred curtain in the bar window, Angela lapsed into silence beside him. M had warned against silence in company, as creating a space for questions, but all her energy seemed to have gone into bracing herself for the coming assault, leaving her too weary to make the effort which in any case was perhaps no longer worth making. She hadn't even the strength, the optimism, to get up, to say goodbye to Alan Boyce and move away from him . . .

'How long are you here for?' Angela had an idea that once again he had had to ask the question twice, and she made a second effort to pull herself together.

'Oh, I don't think we've decided yet,' she said, trying to look open and confiding. A phrase was in her head, a proud slogan: *We never closed*. It was as if she was suddenly wound up again. 'We're always like this on holiday, perhaps because everything's so predictable at home.'

Into her own trap. Clever but not too clever, Gerald had advised—was it only last night? Oh, God, where was Gerald?

'Predictable?'

'Well, you know what I mean. One's time is fairly obviously accounted for in everyday life, isn't it? I mean—although you may not know *precisely* what you'll be doing this time next week, you've got a pretty good idea where you'll be doing it and what sort of thing it'll be. Now—I don't know at this moment, whether or not I shall be sitting here like this, or—or looking out over the plain of Arles.'

Or lying dead.

'Well, don't look so miserable about it.'

'I'm not.' Surreptitiously she grasped the bar counter. 'It's this head.'

172

'You poor little thing.'

He really was looking at her with sympathy. He made her think of a nice mongrel dog who would distract her, if he could, by fetching and carrying sticks.

'Oh, it'll pass.'

With a way of life. *Where were they?*

She heard a noise in the doorway and whirled around. An old man in a panama hat was shuffling past. In the window where the curtain stirred, Angela could see him move slowly among the terrace tables, disappearing at last into the speckled shade.

'Come down to the beach?' suggested Alan.

'No, thanks.' She felt a tiny flicker of Caroline fire. 'Sun isn't exactly the best thing for a hangover. Didn't you know?'

'I'm sorry,' said Alan Boyce humbly, 'I wasn't thinking.'

'And besides,' she said, more kindly, 'I'd better wait and see what the others are doing. Mother, at any rate.'

'Ask her.' Alan nodded beyond Angela and again she jerked round. Mother was at the far end of the long bar. She was glancing over her shoulder, talking animatedly to someone not yet in sight. She looked gay, pretty—even young.

With a second lurch of delight Angela saw that the person following Mother into the bar was Gerald. It was all she could do not to run across to them, but she heard herself call out a lazy 'Hi!' and merely waved an arm. Alan was on his feet.

They came straight across, and she scanned their faces with covert anxiety, looking for a shadow, or a reserve. But both of them seemed more spontaneous than usual, and Mother leaned forward to kiss Caroline's cheek.

'Darling,' she murmured.

Angela was hard put to it not to flinch, from shame. Without the memory of last night, how happy she would be at this moment!

'Dearest Mother . . .'

'I'm sorry I failed to make my usual call.' Mother looked round at them almost roguishly. 'I felt *terribly* lazy . . .'

'I was all set to send you on your way alone this morning,' said Caroline.

'Great minds . . .' said Peter, tweaking her ear. Angela quickly shut out thoughts of Daddy, whose habit this was.

'Where's Father?'

'He went walking *hours* ago. I thought he'd be back by now.'

Why wasn't he back?

'What did you do last night after we saw you?' demanded Alan. Gerald helped Mother on to a stool, drew one up for himself. Alan sat down again.

'A little gambling . . .' Gerald spread his arms out, smiling ruefully. He looked round the bar. 'I don't see your fiancée.'

'No, she's on the beach.'

'Well, then, stay and have a drink with us,' suggested Mother graciously. Angela saw Gerald give her a swift look.

'Thanks most awfully.'

Alan actually said that. He was as cliché-ridden, in his way, as M . . . In the light of her behaviour, Angela shied off thoughts of M, with a sickening penalty in her stomach. Where was Father?

'Caroline?'

'Just soda water please, Mother. I rather overdid it last night.'

Mother's graciousness perhaps increased, Gerald grinned. Angela, from love and guilt, looked down at the bar counter. Every nuance of this easy relationship throbbed through her in its achievement. It was as if they had reached their pitch of creative artistry at the very moment in which she was to destroy it.

Or was she? Mother and Gerald were beside her. Father was out for a walk.

Barbara and her parents had left. The sun was shining.

A great wave of lightness and relief flooded in. How ridiculously intense could you get? She took a deep breath. Alan said:

'You're feeling better.'

'Yes.' She sipped the soda water. Its sparkle had the kick of champagne. 'It's like leaving off banging your head against a wall.'

'Whoever would do that? I mean, whoever would start banging his head against a wall in the first place?' Alan's smile really was invariable.

'Most of us, at some time or another,' said Gerald. He was so handsome this morning, lime cravat under his strong brown chin, long legs in immaculate white trousers, thick shining hair, the old Angela-awe was strong on her. Alan beside him—as most men—gave the impression that nature had been niggardly, although Alan on his own could be seen to be tall, if slight. The only thing Angela liked better about Alan was his laugh—so gentle, so *amused*, so unexpected against the cheerful inanities of his conversation.

'Good morning, sir.' Alan was looking beyond Angela with keen interest and his friendly smile. He sprang to his feet. She turned round as Father's hand came down on her shoulder, and put her own up to touch it. Father looked very warm, but serene.

'I hope you're drinking,' he said.

They all had another one. Father mopped his forehead, and talked about the long walk he had taken up behind the town. The conversation then widened to include the South of France more generally. Angela was fascinated by Mother and Father's elegiac duet on the vanished elegances of the Côte d'Azur. She wondered whether they really felt the nostalgia they expressed so well, or had merely learned it from their sheets of paper. Whatever the truth, the topic comfortably lasted the second drink, and Alan learned nothing about the family Thompson. Nor did they learn anything about Alan—but only, Angela felt, because Mother and Father had so firmly retained the conversational reins. She wondered how Alan would tackle departure, but it was Gerald who tackled it. As he finished his drink he got down from his stool.

'I'll walk along with you and deliver you back to your fiancée. It's a bit early yet for lunch and I've had no exercise this morning'—'Darling!' murmured

Mother—'Anybody else coming?' He looked amused.

Angela didn't really want to leave the sanctuary of the hotel but Mother said: 'We'll all come!'

Angela found she had acquired the habit of looking for Barbara and menacing men, but she saw nothing among the slow-moving colourful crowd to alarm her. She decided though to confide in Gerald after lunch, let him tell her not to worry about a danger that had passed.

They strolled along the Croisette, on the side near the sea, looking down on the beaches.

Alan and Winifred had umbrellas towards the old harbour. Angela was more and more aware of Le Suquet beyond and above them, getting closer. Insubstantial in the daily distance, already it had become a lure. She was beside Gerald as they walked along.

'Peter.' She took his hand. 'I want to go there.' She nodded towards the hill. She could now see the road zigzagging up the face of it, the small gardens hanging in the bends, the varied details of the old houses. 'One afternoon, Peter'—she was whispering—'instead of lying down—when everyone else is lying down—can we climb up there? Wouldn't you like to climb up there?'

Gerald's hand lay passive in hers. He murmured:

'Perhaps. Yes, I would like it.'

Mother came up on Gerald's other side. Alan had stopped and was peering over the rail.

'There she is!'

Angela saw Winifred sitting sideways on to the sea, her arms clasped round her knees, looking up at them with a tolerant smile. Her skin was flecked with water. She must be within the statutory fifteen minutes that followed bathing. Alan was waving anxiously.

'I can see you,' called Winifred lazily.

'Come down?' suggested Alan to the Thompsons.

'I don't think so, thank you. I think we'll be getting back.' Mother took Father's arm. Caroline stood beside Peter. Angela hoped they looked a nice little family. She said in her head, gloomily:

'You will not look upon their like again,' but really for effect. She had ceased, almost, to worry.

'I say, thanks awfully for the drinks,' said Alan, one foot on the stairway that led down to his portion of beach.

'A pleasure,' said Mother, and each of them nodded and smiled and started to walk away. It was so much easier, their leaving Alan than he leaving them.

They strolled amicably back to the hotel, relief flowing in Angela like blood after severe cramp—a relief which swelled and swelled in the growth of family feeling which seemed, now, to be the one real effect of last night's gala and gambling, and which had reached new heights in the face of their combined hospitality to Alan Boyce.

The mood persisted during lunch, and at the end of the meal Gerald said:

'What's the consensus of opinion on sis and me forgoing our sleep this afternoon and exploring Le Suquet?'

Caroline said, in a little girl voice:

'Please, Mother! Please, Father!'

But a shadow fell fast over Mother's face and Gerald went on quickly:

'Perhaps you'd like to come with us, Mother? Perhaps that would be—better? I didn't suggest it as I thought perhaps it would be too hot for you . . .' He stumbled to a halt. Angela had never imagined that Gerald could stumble to a conversational halt. This was the first time he had made her realise in his behaviour that his freedom of choice was as limited as her own.

Always, before, it was as if he knew the bounds and refrained from testing them, bearing himself proudly and comfortably inside them, in the semblance of a free man. But Mother had looked thoroughly put out.

Father said, amiably enough, and not looking at Mother:

'Yes, why don't the three of you go?'

Angela said to Mother, eagerly:

'If you don't want so long a walk, we'll be back in good time for you and me to have our usual stroll,' then winced before the coldness of Mother's eyes.

Gerald leaned over and put his hand on Mother's where it lay on the table. Angela remembered her own experience of doing this, but now Mother didn't recoil.

'What is it, old love? Do you really mind us climbing up Le Suquet in the heat of the day—like Englishmen or mad dogs?' He trapped her in the radiance of his smile and she blinked uncertainly. Angela wondered about Gerald and his own Mother. At least he understood the ideal of the mother/son relationship.

'If you'd really rather we didn't go, of course we won't,' she said, but crossing her fingers under the table.

'No.' Mother gently withdrew her hand and wiped the corners of her mouth with her napkin. Her face wore once again its usual expression of indifferent placidity. 'Off you go, both of you. And'—looking at Angela—'don't hurry back, I'll take a longer rest this afternoon.'

'Thank you, Mother.'

The four of them went upstairs together, divided two by two on the landing. Outside her door Angela turned to Gerald.

'Peter, will you come in a moment?'

He raised one eyebrow and followed her in silence into the room and she closed and locked the door. She sat on the bed and motioned him to a chair. Looking at her quizzically, he slowly sat down. She found herself trembling again and had to grip her hands together.

'I've got to speak out of character,' she said, 'because last night I—acted out of character. Oh, Gerald, I saw a girl from school in the ladies' cloakroom and before I realised—I said hello to her. I know it was terrible, I knew the next *second*. And I didn't have to do it, she wasn't sure until I smiled at her, it would have worked. Oh, Gerald.' He was looking at her without expression, and she hurried on. 'I was lucky, though. She was going away this morning, she and her parents, their holiday was over. So it'll be all right, and I could never be such an idiot a second time . . . Gerald?'

She waited for the reassurance, but it didn't come. He said very quietly:

'Where were they staying?'

'The Miramar. I was just about paralytic with horror, but I did learn that much!'

'And she knows where you are?'

'No! She was doing all the talking, and anyway I pulled myself together.' There was silence. Behind Gerald's motionless head and shoulders the sun shone brilliantly on to her balcony railings, the swallows wheeled and cried in the blue space of the window. Gerald was very pale. 'Gerald, I feel dreadful at having put us all in danger in such a cretinous way. I'd had a bit too much to drink, I think. Not that that excuses anything . . . Gerald, need we tell them? Barbara said they were leaving this morning . . .'

'I think,' Gerald began, speaking slowly and carefully and making Angela think he was trying not to show her his anger, 'that we shall have to tell them, they'll have to check for sure that the danger really is past . . .' and then she interrupted him by screaming his name, because the door opposite, the door that connected with the room which was not his, was slowly but unmistakably opening. Gerald followed her terrified glance and swung round, and

183

suddenly Gypsy was in the room, Gypsy in palest cream shantung, his black hair shining, a gun in his hand.

When he saw Gerald he put the gun away and grinned.

'So it was his master's voice. Sorry, but I can't be too careful.'

'Gypsy . . .'

Tears had welled up and were rolling down her cheeks. Gypsy's grin vanished. He looked from her to Gerald.

'What's the trouble?'

Gerald got up and faced Gypsy with his arm round Angela's shoulders.

'There was an incident. She spoke to someone she knew.' He said to her gently: 'Are you close friends? Where does she live?'

'We're not friends at all and we don't have friends in common. She lives in Liverpool.'

'Name and address and anything else I should know!' ordered Gypsy, his eyes on Gerald.

Angela told him the little she knew about Barbara Shaw. Gerald said, still gently:

'I think you'd better stay here for the time being. We'll postpone Le Suquet.'

He squeezed her shoulders and the two men went respectively through the two connecting doors. She heard the doors close and then she lay down on the bed and curled up tight. She felt as bad as she had felt in the morning, she felt life was a continuous nightmare. There was just one thread of hope: if what she had done could be kept from Mother and Father . . . If Gypsy found, when he checked, that the danger really was negligible, perhaps he needn't tell them. But perhaps Special Branch had rules. Of course Special Branch, above all organisations, had rules. But rules could be bent sometimes, harmlessly, it was like white lies . . .

Angela didn't know how long she had lain on her bed when she heard a door open. She shot upright, huddling against the wall. Gypsy was standing in his doorway again, looking at her the way he used to look during the harder moments of her training, only with a new edge of contempt.

'Gypsy . . .' She put out her hand. He didn't move. He said coldly:

'You're lucky.'

'Oh, Gypsy!'

'Fred Bates and Joe Gunter arrived this morning from England. Terribly amusing coincidence.' Angela thought it was Mother he was mimicking.

'Yes . . . Gypsy, I've done all you've taught me—until last night. Truly I have.

I've been Caroline. No problems. Just last night . . . Mr Bates, I knew what I'd done as soon as I'd done it. I was as horrified as you are. It'll never happen again.'

'It had better not.'

He had never looked more grim, more like a tiger.

'Mr Bates—you don't have to tell them, do you—Mother and Father? You know I'll never be so silly again. Mr Bates of Petersham—Gypsy—need you tell them?'

Gypsy laughed abruptly, showing his crowd of gold-flecked teeth, and the harshness had gone from his face. But he said:

'Doll, they must be told. They already know something's up.'

The knock on the outer door came as if on cue. Gypsy went across and unlocked it, and Mother and Father and Peter came in, followed by Joe. Angela looked down at her knees, drawn up under her chin at the top of the bed. She couldn't look at her parents, only at their legs as they walked past. There was something indecent in seeing them outside their roles, in facing them as the two strangers they really were—like catching them naked.

'For God's sake, what is this?' asked Father. His voice sounded quite different, thin and harsh. Angela was unable to check a shuddering sob, but they ignored her.

She saw Mother's legs settle themselves in front of one of the chairs. She heard Gypsy say:

'It's nothing, now. But I'd better report. The young lady met a friend.'

'A friend!' Mother's voice was different too, high and sharp. Angela at last looked up. Mother's eyes were very wide open and there was a red blob in each sallow cheek. Father was pale. Angela said, her eyes flickering from one to the other of them:

'Please—let me tell you. Last night, in the ladies' loo—I met someone from school. I—spoke to her—as Angela.'

Father advanced to the bed. There was no doubt, now, that his eyes were on her.

'You *what?*'

'Spoke to her.' It was a relief to have confessed it. Angela made herself meet and hold his eyes. 'I knew the next second what I'd done. It'll never happen again. If I hadn't been such an idiot it would have worked, she wasn't sure.' The silence was dreadful, the cold stares. 'She's gone now, back to England.'

There was a terrible moment when Father lifted his hand. But he let it fall, and turned away to the window. Mother said irritably to Gypsy:

'Fred?'

'I went to the Miramar . . .'

'Barbara was staying at the Miramar. She didn't know where I was staying. I'm sorry . . .'

'Be quiet! Go on, Fred.'

'They'd checked out, as our young lady predicted. Back to Blighty on the lunch-time flight from Nice. Three of them—mother, father and daughter. Live in Liverpool. Not a friend of the girl's. No friends in common.'

'So the girl wouldn't appear to have done any damage.' Father spoke without turning round. Angela winced and looked back at her knees. It was absurd to be hurt by a man she didn't know, repudiating a relationship which didn't exist. But she was hurt.

'Nope.' There was a rasping sound, and Angela smelt a new sharp wave of Gypsy's tobacco. She realised that it had won the contest with Mother's perfume, even before he lit this latest cigarette, and a hysterical giggle turned her next sob into a hiccup.

'The arm of coincidence is very long,' murmured Mother, 'but I scarcely think . . .'

There was a silence.

'We have been luckier than she deserves,' said Father's dry voice, at last, almost in its normal tones.

Angela slowly raised her head. Only Gerald was looking at her—with the look of sadness she had seen before, which he suppressed as she met his eye. Joe and Gypsy had their old air, from the flat, of standing to attention, Gypsy in his own negligent fashion, Joe with his empty eyes on space.

Angela, feeling they might now be awaiting her own words on the subject, said:

'Forgive me, please. I've put us in the most dreadful danger, just through being stupid. Nothing like it will happen again, so please don't stop trusting me . . .' She couldn't call them anything because she didn't know, any more, who they were.

At first it was as if the silence had never been broken. Then Mother got to her feet and said:

'Very well. Fred, will you stay and explain to Caroline what the arrival of you and Joe signifies.' She looked coldly at Angela. 'You had better remain in your room until dinnertime, Caroline. Pull yourself together.'

'Yes, Mother, oh, yes!' Angela slid down from the pillow and stretched out on the bed.

Mother turned to Father. 'Caroline must not be given so much to drink in future.'

Mother, Father and Gerald went out. Gerald didn't look at her again. Joe went through the connecting door, shutting it behind him. Angela and Gypsy were alone and looking at each other. Gypsy sat down on the edge of the bed, his hands between his knees, the smoke spiralling up. Angela began to tremble.

'Gypsy, I can't stop trembling.'

'Take it easy, doll.' He was frowning down at the floor.

'Gypsy, I'm so glad to see you. I've been looking forward . . .'

His head jerked up. 'Have you, doll!'

'Yes, Gypsy!' Although only at the briefest, rarest moments had she glimpsed the reason for her excitement, like light into a crack.

He turned suddenly and ground his cigarette out in the ashtray beside the bed, put a hand each side of her body and leaned over her. She could see dark flecks in his fierce blue eyes. His red underlip was so near it was a blur.

I know a lady in Venice would have walked barefoot to Palestine for a touch of his nether lip.

The strange excitement crowded out all other feelings.

'Gypsy . . .'

'Mr Bates, if you please,' said Gypsy. 'You shout "Hello" out there on the terrace tonight before your dinner. Surprised but not surprised. Mr Bates and Mr Gunter will join you for a drink, maybe one night they'll join you for dinner, they'll pass a polite time of day if they meet you in town, or on the beach. That's the form, Miss Thompson.'

'Of course. I shan't make any more mistakes.'

But now he was close to her, at this moment she was looking into his face, his hands were to each side of her on the bed. One of them had once covered her mouth and nose. Treebark and tobacco . . . A touch of his nether lip . . . She was so tired. Shock and strain. Mother had been right. Have a rest, Caroline. But don't go yet, Gypsy, Mr Bates.

Out of the dreamlike peace which now surrounded her she could no longer resist the impulse to—what was it Caroline was going to do?—put her hand up and lay it along the blurred edge of his cheek. 'I'm sorry . . .'

'Go to sleep, doll.'

Gypsy's face came so near it disappeared and took the light with it. She felt it against hers, damp. Angela held her breath and consciously experienced it there, Gypsy's cheek against hers. It was strange, she could remember every occasion when she had come into physical contact with Gypsy . . .

When their mouths met the shock of it sent waves of sensation round her body. But Gypsy drew quickly away, and she saw him again, looking at her hard but without expression, felt the clammy cold on her cheek where his face had been. Had it really?

Horrified, elated, she turned her head against the coverlet and closed her eyes.

Gypsy said gently:

'Go to sleep, now, doll. Don't worry. Nothing's going to happen to you.' He laughed, rather strangely.

'Thank you, Mr Bates.'

She felt the bed react to the loss of Gypsy's weight. She didn't open her eyes again. She heard the connecting door click open and shut, then a key turn. Disappointment, relief, excitement and shame

192

ran together like wax features in a fire, and she slept.

— CHAPTER 9 —

Angela slept heavily, and when she awoke the square of glass in the balcony door was coloured navy blue. The drama of the afternoon already seemed a long way off, but the chairs stood in unaccustomed places and she had itchy eyelids and a stuffy nose.

She put on her plainest dress, and noted with satisfaction that despite the cosmetic properties of a tanned skin her eyes still looked red and swollen, and her nose unnaturally broad. She spoke aloud to her reflection. She said: 'Caroline, you are an incorrigibly hopeless creature', to see if her voice held the catarrhal aftermath of tears, and thought that it did.

She realised how hot and tired her head was when, dressed for the evening, she stood on the balcony and felt the coolness of the air. It was now quite dark, and the points of light edging the coast under the Esterels were so near she felt she could have hit one of them with a pebble. A tiny star lay close to the huge full moon and was almost eclipsed by it. Large moon, small star, blinkered human point of view!

Angela decided that star-gazing, during terrestrial stress, was beneficial. She even shrugged off the disappointment of looking at her watch and seeing, by the light of the moon, that Gerald would not now be coming to call for her on his way down. By leaning dangerously far over the balcony, she thought she could just glimpse the family group on the terrace below.

When she got downstairs they were there in the usual place, Mother and Father and Peter, and an empty chair. Murmuring 'Hello', Caroline took her seat. As always, when she reached the table, Father and Peter half rose. Mother said kindly:

'Better, dear?' And Caroline with a lift of the heart replied:

'Very much better, thank you, Mother. I slept for quite a while, and my headache's almost gone.'

'That's good, dear.'

Mother looked her usual self, and once again Angela couldn't be sure if Father's vague smile was on her or on the scene in general. Peter said 'Sis, you've just missed a prize tableau', and described a small drama whose bizarre *dramatis personae* had obligingly halted for its enactment on the other side of the low wall that separated the Thompson table from the pavement of the Croisette. A waiter brought a cinzano and set it in front of her.

It seemed that the gap was closed.

But things were no longer exactly as they had been. Mr Bates and Mr Gunter were strolling along towards them from the direction of Palm Beach.

Angela, watching the two figures approaching, one tall, one short, one moving with long lazy stride, the other trotting to keep pace with him, marvelled at the efficient stage management of Special Branch, which never revealed its mechanics front of house. So much had happened behind the scenes that afternoon, but the curtain had gone up on the evening performance to reveal no more than a family having drinks on a hotel terrace and two acquaintances from home ambling up to exchange greetings.

When Gypsy and Joe came abreast of the Thompsons' table Gypsy vaulted the low wall and Joe looked at it, then walked on to the gateway and came in that way. Angela was still trying not to giggle while chairs were being dragged up and the party expanded. Gypsy said, 'Good evening, Miss Thompson' and Joe nodded to her.

Father, on the hearty side, was asking them about their journey, comparing it with his own. When he looked round for the waiter, Mother already had him at her side. All were given drinks except for Caroline, but her glass anyway was still half full and omission was managed without comment, so that Angela didn't think Gypsy and Joe, if things had been as they appeared, would have noticed she was the only one not to be replenished. So persuasive of reality was Father's welcome that for a few minutes Angela forgot that both Mr Bates and Mr Gunter had heard Mother's directive about Caroline's future drinking—that Mr Bates had actually been instrumental in bringing it about. Savouring the situation, she found she had recovered her old excitement at the sheer ingenuity of the charade.

After a few moments of general conversation, Father wondered aloud, with a new hesitation and delicacy, when he was going to see Mr Bates and Mr Gunter up at the house, and Mr Bates said a visit to White Gates was top of the list for new jobs when they got back home. Angela wondered if it was a code, if Father really was learning something to his satisfaction. She found it very agreeable and relaxing, after being the centre of so many dramas in so short a time, to sit back probably unnoticed and watch and listen and try to spot the real betraying itself through the elaborate unreality—betraying itself through a tic in a cheek, a vein in a temple, a sudden too sharp movement, a too intense stare . . .

'Hello again!'

Alan's cheerful face was on the far side of the wall, and she realised how tired she was, how little she wanted to bother. Winifred Holland was beside him, holding his hand, in a yellow Angela-dress which Caroline saw as rather a pity.

'Good evening,' said Father, midway between the heartiness with which he had greeted Gypsy and Joe, and the quiet confidentiality into which his voice had sunk.

'We weren't wanting to disturb you,' said Alan brightly, 'although we were hoping to see you. We wanted to ask you, you know . . . No, thanks'—as Gypsy held a cigarette packet out towards him—'I used to smoke but I hardly ever do these days and . . .'

'We wanted to ask you to join us for a drink,' said Winifred, laying a finger on Alan's lips. He said eagerly, when she took it away:

'Yes. Yes, that's it!'

'I'm afraid we . . .'

'Oh, not now, necessarily,' said Winifred. 'Are you engaged all evening?'

'What were you thinking of, Miss er . . . ?' asked Mother.

'Do you know Magali on the Croisette?' asked Winifred. 'Opposite the gardens, and there's a concert on tonight. Full-blown orchestral concert. Could you meet us there, later?'

'That sounds very pleasant,' murmured Mother.

'Very pleasant,' said Father.

'And if we find ourselves, we old people,' sighed Mother, 'feeling too tired after dinner—French meals tend to be such *prolonged* affairs, don't they?'—'Oh, pleasantly prolonged, Mother!' protested Caroline—'If we find ourselves when the time comes wanting to retire to our beds, well then, I'm sure the children will be very happy to join you.'

'Really, Mother!' said Caroline.

'Oh, we'll all come,' said Peter, 'they won't be tired. See you at a table outside Magali's—half past nine?'

'I say, that'll be splendid!' said Alan, and stood there smiling at them until Mother said, 'Oh, excuse me!' and introduced them to Mr Bates and Mr Gunter. Mother had to be reminded of Alan's and Winifred's names. After the introductions

198

Winifred tucked her arm into Alan's and marched him off.

Angela took a sip of her cinzano. Above their heads some dry palm leaves rattled, and she pulled her shawl on to her shoulders because it felt, if only for a moment, as if the warm dark shawl of the night had been lifted off and left her aware that she could be cold. Mother gave a small shiver.

Father said, in a eureka tone:

'Magali's! It *has* got a good reputation! Let's have dinner there—and be on the spot for Caroline's friends.'

'Not especially my friends,' said Caroline. Father sounded as if he had seized on Magali's to get out of dining with Messrs Bates and Gunter without being rude. Of course, dinner together was not envisaged for that evening, but if things had been what they seemed the Thompsons would have had to tackle the situation with tact. Angela wondered if even Mother and Father had begun to play the game for its own sake, seeing that the feelings of Messrs Gunter and Bates didn't really need to be considered. But someone could always be listening—at least that was the only safe presumption on which to proceed.

'The food in the hotel is excellent,' said Father. 'We dine here, as often as not.'

'We'll dine here tonight,' said Gypsy. He leaned back in his chair with the familiar flopping motion. His eyes roved round and found Angela. Stayed with her.

'And how is Miss Thompson enjoying herself? What are you doing with yourself these days, Miss Thompson?'

Mischief lurked in his eyes. What relish he seemed to get from everything he did! A half thought gave Caroline an involuntary shiver . . . Gypsy was, apparently, a business acquaintance of her father, but they all knew better, they knew that he was her creator. How mean he was! But perhaps he, too, was beginning to admire the creation for its own sake. Angela, from her relaxed, semi-spectator status, was uncomfortably on her toes.

'At this moment, Mr Bates, I'm enjoying myself very much indeed. You wouldn't be so unkind as to push me into thoughts of the real, earnest world, would you?'

Gypsy shifted in his chair, in one of his extravagant movements. There was an enormous contrast between the leisured way he had of throwing his body about, and his economy of movement when he was holding a gun.

'Oh, Miss Thompson, I wouldn't be unkind to you at all, I assure you!'

Angela thought there might be admiration in his eyes, at the way she had taken his challenge. She felt euphorically happy. She could perhaps become dependent on this charade, like a drug.

'I'm relieved to hear it, Mr Bates!' There was no need to say any more, but Angela thought she would be sporting. 'No, actually, I shall have to start thinking about fixing myself up with a secretarial course when we get back—but I shall, I hope, contrive to postpone it until the autumn.'

Angela listened to Caroline's running accompaniment of giggle with only the mildest feelings of contempt. Caroline was someone to be reckoned with after all, she could teach Angela things which were better learnt.

Mr Bates was suddenly not interested in Miss Thompson's reluctant plans for the future. Either she had passed his test, or he was hungry, or the time had come for the inexorable next phase. He was on his feet, and a second later so was Mr Gunter.

'Well, thanks,' said Gypsy, and Joe nodded. 'We'll be on our way to dinner now. See you around.'

The Thompsons moved off too, slowly along the Croisette. They found a table on the pavement outside Magali: not right on the edge, where people knocked the tall menu cards over as they squeezed past, and every itinerant Arab spread his armful of bangles, but against the window frame of the restaurant. So that they once again, in a sense, had their backs to the wall and could look out in each direction around them, and inwards to the quiet unpopular interior of the café, where the only customers were an old man wearing his napkin like a bib, and a pair of amorous teenagers in a corner.

Outside all was animation, and waiters nimbly negotiating the narrow network of gaps which was their freeway. The meal was good, and Caroline was given a glass of the rather special red wine which Father ordered, and of which he and Mother drank freely. Peter had a couple of glasses.

But despite the abundance of the meal, and the wine, Angela had to pull her shawl round her again, the first evening she had needed it. What was it? There was something . . . She looked across the road. Were the palms and pines chattering more excitedly than usual? The sea was as quiet as ever it was, the sky as remotely clear. She could see Le Suquet in its unreflective orange glow, a glow that illuminated no more than the church tower and the roofs immediately below it, isolating them in a darkness which was the more dense and velvety where it met the golden aureole.

Father drained the last of his wine and lit a rare cigar.

'Ought you to be smoking that thing with so many people eating?' asked Mother.

'It's all right,' said Father. And indeed, the smoke was being carried steadily upwards and then towards the sea. By what force? There didn't seem to be any wind, although the dry palm leaves still chattered in the moments of silence . . .

There was the tootle of a wind instrument in the clear air. Its serpentine invitation sent a shudder of delight and excitement along Angela's spine. It was followed by other musical strands—the deeper thicker coil of a bassoon, strings tuning, the beat of a drum.

'It's the music!' said Alan, appearing at the table with Winifred in tow. 'Would you like to go over, have a drink afterwards?'

'You would!' said Caroline.

'I would too.' Gerald got to his feet and helped Mother up. Father settled the bill and they threaded between the tables to the pavement edge, and eventually got across the road. Deck-chairs and upright chairs had been arranged in rows in front of the clearing where the orchestra was assembled, at right angles to the sea. From the seats they were able to find together, near the front, they looked across the musicians to Le Suquet above them.

As the conductor, with raised shoulders and baton, glanced round his silent poised players, Angela heard the palm fronds chattering with a new agitation. And then the conductor dropped his baton and music swelled out into the night, music which swirled round her, took her from before and behind and on each side, and the eye and the ear, for once in life, played their ordained complementary roles as Le Suquet, calm and benign above the musical battle, became a symbol of its quest.

Rather to Angela's surprise Alan whispered 'Overture: *La Forza del Destino*', and then words, too, took their place with the sound and the picture, and they seemed the most thrillingly appropriate words that Angela had ever heard, for that moment, in that place, into the sweet and shivering uncertainty of her mind and body. She even felt that if the men who killed other men were to find her now and despatch her she would no longer be regretful or even afraid, she would die in a sort of triumph at dying while her perceptions were at their height, a tragic figure because all the jostling possibilities of her young life would never be realized, and because one day someone, somewhere, would say over her memory, in that most poignantly dismissive of phrases: 'But that was in another country; and besides, the wench is dead.' (But what was Marlowe's context? Fornication, wasn't it?)

Angela sat there rapt through the overture, and into the beginning of the symphony, in harmony with herself and the universe and aware of the rarity of the experience. Whatever came afterwards, whatever pleasures or pains, the present for once was complete.

And then suddenly a flurry of white paper blew up in the conductor's face, and he grabbed and dabbed at it like somebody trying to catch a fly, and it escaped him, and he spreadeagled his hand over the remaining paper on his rostrum and tried to go on conducting. But a big sheet of score flapped by almost within reach of her, Angela thought from one of the violins, and a music stand crashed down, and the conductor took his hand off his music in order to turn over, from long habit, and there was another white whirlwind, which he pursued down the pedestal and out sideways with a balletic leap, until he seemed to be surrounded by fluttering pages, his own and his players', and the music started to limp and to thin out, and the makeshift stage was a mixture of musicians playing gamely on, and musicians making more balletic leaps (like the chorus after the star) or crawling along the ground, and there was paper everywhere.

The last notes didn't die away into silence, they died into a continuous muffled shriek and insistent clatter of palm leaves. The canvas seats of the empty deck-chairs were straining upwards like round bellies in candy stripes, Angela's hair was whipping her ears and her forehead, her shawl hardly seemed enough to snuggle into and must be held tight in both hands. Only Le Suquet, it seemed, was still at rest. Gerald roared out 'Mistral!' and the orchestra redoubled its frenzied efforts to recover its music, and suddenly they were all laughing, at first sniggering, rather ashamed and each of them trying to keep it unnoticed by the others, then openly and uproariously, because the sudden disruption was as magnificently funny as the music had been magnificently solemn.

Alan Boyce called out, 'Over the road!' and they scrambled up and crossed the road as quickly as the traffic allowed, holding desperately on to everything which wasn't attached, and even Mother's hair was blown out of place.

'In here!' somebody shouted, and they were inside the café that had so recently been empty, just managing to get a table in the window as it began to fill up, looking out at the deserted tables on the pavement and seeing a waiter chasing a paper table cloth into the road.

'What a pity!' said Winifred, and they all started to laugh again, in a sort of exhilaration, Angela thought, that was not so far removed from her recent exaltation, merely another aspect of it. Across the road they could just glimpse the continuing chaos among the trees, darting figures and small light-coloured objects tossing through the air.

'So *quickly*,' murmured Mother, a mirror in her hand, anxiously studying her hair.

'That's how it happens,' said Winifred. Angela had an idea that the Mistral experience was a new one for Mother, casting doubts on the authenticity of her Riviera lament.

'What will you all drink?' demanded Alan. It was a different world, inside the café, under the weak yellow lights, looking out on the empty pavements and the wildly waving palms. Beyond, the sea creamed, lights in the street creaked and swayed. It was cool enough for the women to need their wraps.

In the grip of her strange excitement Angela was only gradually aware that Winifred was talking to her.

'I'm sorry, I was fascinated by the change in everything.'

The tray of drinks arrived. A *citron pressé* for Angela.

'That was what I was saying—at least, I was saying that you looked excited.'

'Does it show?' But she wasn't really surprised, she felt, inwardly, the life in her face. 'The music started me off, the wind took over.' She studied Winifred's face. Still pale, unrevealing, promising competence. Would Alan Boyce one day feel stifled?

'How long are you staying in Cannes?' asked Winifred.

'I honestly don't know. I think we've booked to the end of the week, but as I said to Alan this morning'—only this morning?—'we could take off tomorrow. Or stay another fortnight. We've got a couple of weeks of holiday still to go.'

Winifred was looking at Alan. Angela wasn't sure whether or not she was listening. She looked somehow untouched by the upheaval of the wind, the only one of them. But her hair was always in a cloud.

'How long will you be here?' *Quid pro quo*, the safe way round.

'Oh, I expect we'll be here another ten days.'

'Then back to work?'

'For me, yes. Alan's on sick leave.'

'Oh, dear. What . . . ?'

'Glandular fever. Sort of on and on. But it's off now. Only it leaves you weak. Granny's place seemed the answer.'

'I haven't got to get back to work,' said Angela, 'but I must start a secretarial course by the autumn at the latest. Worse luck. What do you do, Winifred?'

'Secretarial work,' said Winifred complacently, and Angela realised with a sense of freedom that when she went back to England she would not be taking a secretarial course. When she went . . . if she went . . . She was getting soft. Since luck had saved her earlier in the day she had had no sense of danger. But nothing had changed, and as if to underline their situation there was a loud report from the street.

Only a backfire, but looking swiftly towards her family, Caroline thought her father's hand had moved to the breast of his jacket.

A swirl of sharp-tasting motor fuel spun in through the window, its grey twists climbing towards the yellow lights. In the street a group of boys and girls were yelling in the excitement of the gale.

Mother refused Alan's suggestion of another drink and got up. 'We're going to leave you now,' she said, 'if you will excuse us.' She glanced at Father, who got up too. She looked from Gerald to Angela, thoughtfully. 'You come when you're ready.'

'Oh, I say, what a pity, you're quite sure . . . ?'

'Quite sure, thank you,' said Mother. She walked briskly to the door, then cowered there, fluttering her hands above her head. A moment later, Angela saw Mother and Father climbing into a taxi, Mother's head swathed in chiffon. There would always be a taxi available when Mother wanted one.

The café now was full of people, all talking rather loudly and animatedly in the common experience of the Mistral. Gerald bought drinks. He didn't ask Angela what she wanted, just ordered her a cinzano. Alan, shaking off his slight gloom at being overruled about payment, said enthusiastically:

'I say, how about our having a day out, the four of us, going a bit further afield? Then you could come back to the villa for dinner.'

'That would be nice,' said Winifred. 'Granny loves visitors.'

'Where did you think of going?' Gerald asked. Angela liked the idea but felt slightly afraid of it. Not, of course, that she thought Alan and Winifred could be members of the granite-faced gang, but of the idea of escaping, if only for a few hours, from the routine they had devised to make life as safe as possible in the midst of danger.

'Have you been to the *Fondation Maeght?*' asked Alan eagerly, and Winifred sniffed.

'Your fiancée is reserved on the subject of the *Fondation Maeght.*'

'What is it?' asked Angela.

'It's a sort of shrine to modern art,' said Winifred distastefully. 'Papier mâché statues in the grounds, daubs on the walls, in and out. But in the most dazzling hilly spot near St Paul. The landscape is beautiful *despite* the Fondation. The outdoor exhibits made me think of a neglected fairground. But never mind, it's interesting.'

'I rather like it,' said Alan apologetically. 'And at least everybody will like tea, or drinks, or what have you, in St Paul-de-Vence, and we'd hardly do one without the other.'

'I'd like to go,' said Caroline, but unable to say it without a search of her brother's face. Peter said:

'So should I—when the wind drops. The only thing is—Mother and Father may suddenly suggest a move—it's their way—so we can't cut and dry it. But we'll say "yes" if we're still here when the Mistral's over.'

'Do you know about the Mistral?' Winifred asked Angela. Angela shook her head. 'It blows for one day, or three days, or five, or seven. Always one of that number. No indication in the quality of the wind when it begins to tell you when it will stop. So we shall just have to wait and see.'

Winifred Holland would surely be a very efficient and reliable secretary. The thought of her efficiency made Angela feel tired, and then she realised she had been tired before the thought of Winifred in an office, desperately tired. It had, in fact, one way and another, been the longest day of her life.

'Peter . . .'

He gave her a glance. 'You're *tired*. Even with your brown it shows tonight.'

Winifred was looking at her with a sort of knowing compassion which made Angela feel a bit uneasy. Alan said:

'By jove, yes, and you had a heck of a headache this morning, didn't you? Was it only this morning?'

He might well ask. 'Yes, it was this morning. I agree that it seems a long time ago.'

She and Peter stood up. Out of all the actors in this bizarre drama, Gerald had been the one consistently to understand her, the one who had seemed, at the beginning of things, to be aware of her the least. As if to echo her thoughts, Winifred said:

'Lucky you, to have a brother, and one who looks after you so well.'

'You haven't, then?'

Angela thought Winifred hesitated a moment, but she said, firmly enough,

'No brothers or sisters.'

'Well, you'll soon have a husband to look after you,' said Gerald. Angela thought there might be something dry in his tone. She looked at him quickly, but his face wore its usual expression of polite attention.

'Yes, when are you getting married?' Angela asked.

'We hope September,' said Winifred.

'Oh, lovely . . .' Suddenly Angela laughed and went on laughing. Gerald said softly, 'Take it easy.' Alan said, 'Do let us into the joke.'

'I will.' But it was a few minutes before she could get it out. 'Winifred described tonight's effort as a full-blown concert.' She went on laughing. Alan's anxious polite face seemed even funnier than the joke. So that she wouldn't laugh any more she dug her nails into the palm of her hand. Winifred's lips quivered, but she didn't laugh. The men did, but Gerald took Angela's arm and walked her to the door under cover of the amusement.

As she left the shelter of the doorway she just managed to catch her shawl as it streamed towards the sea. Her hair felt as if it was being blown off, tears started down her face from the outside corners of her eyes. Gerald's thick hair rose and fell like a thatch. Pieces of detached dry palm leaves whirled by. Gerald shouted:

'Get back in the café! I'll find a taxi.'

'No, no!' Angela shouted back to him. 'This is lovely. This is what I want!'

She was full of energy, facing into the onslaught of the clean wind, feeling eyes,

214

ears, nostrils, scalp, honed and invigorated. The puffiness from hours of weeping was subsiding from her eyes, even as the wind brought those tiny new darts of tears to their outer corners.

Gerald took her hand and they began to stride along. Angela kept her head up, taking the wind on her chin. Now she could see the white foam in packed moving lines on the inky sea. The whole of life around them was moving at a spanking pace, as if it had caught movement in the same irresistible, quickening way that things catch fire. The distance to the hotel was too short, and once they were inside, the staircase was too much of a climb. Gerald almost carried her up the last few steps, and along the corridor.

'Give me your key.'

He unlocked the door for her, and when she turned to say goodnight he put his arm across her shoulders and walked her inside, shutting the door. He sat her down on the bed, himself beside her.

'Thank you, Peter,' murmured Caroline. How many times had Angela day-dreamed herself to this point! But Caroline drooped her head on her brother's shoulder, tensing inside, recognising some sort of danger signal, no longer entirely comfortable in his presence.

It was amazing, the different sorts of alerts which could sound in your body—in your throat and your forehead, down the centre of your stomach—it might be the warning of a danger you didn't really want to avert, or the warning of a development which, if permitted, would kill something good and put nothing of value or any real possibility in its place . . .

Gerald's arm tightened across her shoulders, and he turned to look at her. She went on looking straight ahead.

'Are you all right, dear?'

The word 'dear' was very moving, and absolutely astonishing coming from Gerald, but the danger signals were up against it.

'I'm just tired, Peter.'

'I worry about you.'

She thought suddenly of M insulting Gerald in the flat, of Gerald blushing scarlet, and Angela turning away, because it didn't suit him. What was happening now didn't suit him either. *Gerald, don't* . . .

He was studying her face intently, and she felt herself closing something down behind it—behind her eyes, her mouth—presenting only their surface. He said:

'I'll look after you as well as I can.'

'I know you will.'

216

She shifted her weight. She was so tired, so anxious to be alone, but he put his hand up and turned her face towards him. The word 'incest' was an absurd one to think of in this unreal situation. Nevertheless it was in her mind, even when he said, softly:

'Angela.'

Oh, no!

He was kissing her lips, very gently, and she knew it was for her to make what she would of it, but he was kissing the thin tight line that was the mouth of his sister Caroline. She turned her head aside, so that her cheek lay against her brother's. She murmured:

'Peter, dearest Peter, please . . .' and Gerald gave a heavy sigh and drew away from her. She began to cry, quietly and sadly, depressed and regretful, tears poured down her cheeks. She choked to him:

'I am a fool, but today so much has happened. And I'm so tired . . .'

'I know. I know.' He knew it was more than tiredness. 'You're a good, kind girl . . .'

That was what Mother had said, but Angela pushed it angrily aside.

'No! No! You're the good one! The kind one!'

'Don't say that!' He almost shouted, then said softly, 'We'll have that walk to Le Suquet. When the wind drops.'

How generous he was! She loved him best of them all, of course, and yet . . .

He said:

'Will you sleep, do you think?'

'Will I!'

He got to his feet then, and stood looking down at her. He seemed as he always did, contained, proud, free, except that he was pale under the tan and his hair untidy, making him look vulnerable.

Angela got up too, and put her hands on his shoulders. She would love him as long as she lived.

'Goodnight, Peter. God bless.'

'Goodnight, dear.'

He kissed her on both cheeks, *à la française*, and left her.

Lying in bed, having put the light out without reading, Angela, as she slid into sleep, detected a sort of buoyancy and confidence struggling up through her tiredness and self-dissatisfaction. She had acquired something for the long future, something to fall back on, to line her courage with for facing the social jungle of real life. Gerald, whose self-sufficiency had once summed up everything inadequate, everything impossible about Angela, had, in the end, been the one to ask, and she the one to refuse.

So Angela knew now, from experience, that one should never feel certain of failure, any more than of success. .

—— CHAPTER 10 ————————

The Mistral blew for three days. Hotel lounges and lobbies tended to be crowded. Out of doors life took on the jerky rhythm of old movies and nobody lingered or strolled. On the beach the pattern of umbrella globes became a pattern of narrow cones. Mother ceased to go down to the sea, and Angela took long striding walks about the town, revelling in the wind and her solitude (although she always met Mr Bates or Mr Gunter at some point, and sometimes both of them). Eventually she sprinted across the road, weighted her wrap under the mattress, swam in the newly animated sea, and sprinted back to the hotel with sand in her eyes.

She saw Mother for the first time each morning before lunch in the hotel bar. Mother was always there by noon, ready graciously to greet the daughter who erupted into the bar for a moment on her way upstairs to get tidy. Gerald was always there with Mother, paying her a lot of jokey attention, and Angela felt somehow at a disadvantage, getting more instead of less out of breath as she stood for a moment under their kindly smiles. Carrying on upstairs after ordering her invariable *citron pressé*, looking down at her sandalled feet (the varnish needed renewing) and seeing little puffs of sand shoot out from beneath her toes and vanish into the heavy pattern of the carpet (like her sherry in the flat), Angela experienced a sort of jealousy of Gerald's success with Mother, of Mother's evident enjoyment of his attentions. As far as Angela was concerned there had been nothing approaching repetition of the moment in Mother's room when they had been briefly in touch.

While the Mistral blew Angela found it impossible to fall into the suffocating sleep which had eventually claimed her during the hot still afternoons, even while she was resenting her imprisonment and convinced that sleep would never come. Now, she sat upright on her bed, reading *Wives and Daughters* and French novels, staring at the brilliant blue window and the swallows tossed like tea leaves, her ears strained for sounds from either side of her, a strange sensation of waste and regret in her heart. A ridiculous sensation, that things might have happened during those long unoccupied afternoons which would have turned them into pinnacles to look back on for the rest of her life, standing out from the level landscape. But they were ebbing uneventfully away, and would not come again.

How eagerly she awaited Mother's knock! It was like being brought back to life. They scuttled through the gale into what had settled into Mother's favourite café. Her head now was wreathed always in pastel chiffon. She obviously hated the wind. Angela thought her temper had deteriorated under it, if not under the stress of their situation. It wasn't that she had grown noticeably irritable, but Angela could sense that her placidity was imposed with less and less ease on her nervous anxiety, and their silences were no longer the oddly restful experiences they had been at the start. Only when she was being mildly provoked by her son, it seemed to Angela, did Mother relax now.

They no longer browsed from shop to shop: they sat an extra half hour over their tea, and Mother ate two pastries instead of one. While still at the table she decided what she wanted to buy, and they made swift sorties in specific directions.

The wind seemed to curtail so much. No more leisurely drinks on the terrace or along the Croisette cafés after dinner, no more opportunities to observe what was no longer going on at neighbouring tables or under neighbouring umbrellas, no more romantic tree-framed evening settings. Caroline found her thoughts less interesting among the settees and chairs of the hotel lounge. All at once the evenings, which had been too short, began to be too long, no one seemed quite to know what to do with them, and Mother and Father started to go earlier and earlier to bed. One night they went to a restaurant because it was said to have an attractive interior—an aspect of restaurants that had been of no consideration in the other lazy-paced world of dinner under the stars. One evening Mr Bates bought Caroline a *crème de menthe* after dinner, and Peter bought an English version of Scrabble. This was the greatest blessing of the Mistral, and sent Angela and Gerald to bed with slightly stretched minds. Angela hated the thought of judging anyone on his ability to play Scrabble but found it impossible not to, and Gerald made himself even more admired by winning an average of two games out of three, heightening her sense of regret.

The third night of the Mistral they went to the casino again, a decision which seemed to come just in time to rescue them from a gradual individual sinking into boredom and pessimism, back to the communal challenge of their enterprise. They had dinner in the restaurant of the *salle de jeux*, on the raised platform which had seemed to Angela the only section of the *salle* outside the dedicated religiosity of the tables. Now the doors to the terrace were closed, and the backdrop of trees the length of the wall had changed from the still photograph of their first visit into a threshing motion picture.

But the meal was cheerful, even festive. Mother, for a start, was all smiles and delicate coquetry. Perhaps she had simply wanted to go to the casino again.

The routine was the same. Caroline was given three round chips, and the injunction that they would not be staying long. Mother walked out of earshot while Father was pronouncing it, and Gerald laughed, so that she would hear him. Caroline at once turned the three chips into twelve, then into twenty-four. At the third spin of the wheel, absorbed as she was, she noticed a special quality in the silence round the table, and she had to look up, over the attentive heads, towards the expanse of trees and night beyond the window.

The trees were as motionless as the people.

'*Vingt-huit, noir, pair et passe!*'

The stake had gone, but she still had an unwieldy handful of chips. She dropped some as she ran looking for Gerald. An attendant picked them up for her. Gerald appeared as she was thanking him.

'Not another incident?'

'No. *No!* But look!' She pointed towards the outdoors. A couple of waiters were opening the doors onto the terrace. 'Come on!'

Angela pulled Gerald by the hand. The air outside was warm and utterly still. They were strolling again, backwards and forwards in the limited space, re-establishing their summer rhythm. The world was like a slate washed clean, offering a fresh start. Angela turned her chips into francs.

On the way home Mother said:

'We'll go down to the beach in the morning, Caroline. I'll call for you.'

Angela slept well and dreamlessly that night, in the reassurance of the re-established routine, and almost slept again on the beach after she had bathed, just aware of the sun on her body and the resumed stereophonic symphony of human and animal sounds.

'Good morning, Mabel!'

One voice was insistently near, and almost familiar. It was accompanied by a loss of heat. Angela reluctantly opened her eyes and saw Mother looking up with unwonted animation at a man standing in front of them, his large shadow lying across Angela's body. Her eyes fell first on his broad shoulders and heavy freckled chest with its few fair hairs, his narrow hips and short sturdy legs. Then she looked up. The eyes were twinkling in anticipation of meeting hers, there was a broad smile on the wide florid face.

'Uncle Mac!'

Angela's effusive greeting hid a lurch of uneasiness. Whatever else M was bringing with him, he was bringing change. The routine of the seaside, which she had come to enjoy and to rely on, was after all at an end.

Mother said, affectionately:

'You old sinner! So you've made it after all!' and M bent forward to kiss first her, then Caroline.

Mother said, admonishingly:

'Caroline . . .' and Angela struggled to her feet and raised a deck-chair from its lowest to its highest rung, dragging it forward between the two mattresses, into the maximum shade of the umbrella. M sat slowly down, lifting his neat white legs on to the leg rest.

'Well, Mabel, Caroline . . .' He beamed to each side of him. Angela thought he would enjoy his latest role. 'All well, then?'

'Oh, gosh, yes,' said Caroline, as he turned to look at her speculatively. She wondered with another stab of unease if they had told him about her lapse. But if they had, they would have told him too about the rest of it, which they couldn't criticise. She had helped them, successfully, to bring his blueprint to life. 'This is a wonderful place, Uncle Mac,' she said eagerly, 'but then, you know all about that.'

'It's a long time since I was last here, Caroline.'

Had he ever been here, or anywhere, without a purpose?

'I know. And you won't like it so well as you did. Mother doesn't. Or Father. They're always telling us. Have you seen Father and Peter yet?'

'Yes. I saw them at the hotel.'

'You've got in, then,' said Mother. 'You are the luckiest creature.'

'I am lucky,' said Uncle Mac, complacently.

'You always were. I suppose you've been driving all night.'

'No. Only since five o'clock of this morning. I've had a shower and I'm splendid.'

He patted his stomach and Mother sniffed. 'And how long have you decided to give us the pleasure of your company?'

'Oh, I'm only stopping one night, Mabel. I've come to see old Provence. The real thing. I only came down here to say hello to my family. And to try and persuade them—that they might like to move on with me.'

It was the first M pause, and must mean business. Angela's mind's eye saw him behind a desk, fitting his finger-tips together, choosing and savouring words that would alter people's lives.

'Well . . .' murmured Mother, 'we certainly weren't intending to stay here the whole time, as you very well know.'

'So.' M altered his weight distribution, and the chair protested. His shins were already faintly pink below the shadow of the umbrella fringe. 'I've spoken to Bruce and Peter.'

'And what did they say?'

'They said they would leave it to you.'

The irony of it! Or perhaps not, perhaps this was Mother's department. Perhaps. Perhaps.

Mother's mouth pursed. She shook her head. 'I don't know . . .'

She was playing very well the part of a woman who was making up her own mind. 'Caroline?'

Angela jumped. M really was thorough. He appeared to be consulting her.

'Whatever the rest want,' said Angela, rather flatly. Why did they have to move, if not because of danger? Nothing the Thompson family did was without significance. Movement eventually had always been part of the plan, of course, but somehow she hadn't thought it would ever come.

'No enthusiasm, Caroline?' M was beaming at her, but she thought his eyes had lost their sparkle. She said, carefully,

'Oh, Uncle Mac, I'm just embarrassed with *richesses*. Everything's so super I honestly don't mind *what* we do. But of course I should be sorry if we went home and hadn't had a trip into the interior.

'You hear that, Mabel?'

Mother sighed. 'We'll come with you, Mac.'

'That's my girl. Ah!'

Father and Peter were plodding along the soft sands towards them. Angela flicked her towel straight and Gerald sat on it. Mother did the same with hers for Father. She put her hand on his shoulder.

'Under starter's orders, I understand?'

Oh, yes!

Father grinned.

'Only if you wish it.' They must be enjoying the game for its own sake.

'Oh, we'll go.'

Angela looked at M. His head was against the back of the chair, his eyes closed. She said very quietly to Gerald:

'Peter, the last chance, Le Suquet . . .'

'Of course. Leave it to me.'

It was ridiculous, that she should find this so important in the midst of everything else. But she did. She looked at Uncle Mac, and he had turned his head towards her and opened his eyes. The old response to challenge returned.

'The beach here is super, Uncle Mac. Such marvellous sand. And not a single pebble.'

Their eyes met. M shook and rumbled.

'Ah, but very little of it is native sand, Caroline. When the Croisette was widened the narrow beach became even narrower and so they—imported sand.'

'And it stuck.'

'Yes. They must—ah—have employed techniques to ensure . . .'

'Of course.'

Angela looked away from Uncle Mac, across the sea. The Esterels, again, were the vaguest of distant outlines, the separation of sky and sea was visible only when one looked at it askance. How beautiful it was!

'Hello, there!'

The Esterels, the expanse of sparkling sea and Angela's sense of wonder disappeared behind Alan Boyce's smiling face. Winifred was beside him, holding his hand.

'Introduce me!' demanded M, with a playful smile.

'Oh. Uncle Mac, this is Winifred Holland, and her fiancé, Alan Boyce. And this is my Uncle Mac. Mr. McGregor, I suppose I should say, but it sounds so funny. Mother's brother.' They murmured acknowledgements. M waved a hand, and Alan and Winifred squatted on the sand. Gerald gave Winifred most of Angela's towel.

Angela pressed on. 'Alan and Winifred are lucky, Uncle Mac, Winifred's Granny has a villa at Le Cannet. Think of that!'

'You're coming to have dinner with us,' said Alan, and Gerald said immediately on this:

'Sorry, old chap, but the order's come through. Tomorrow we march!'

It was extraordinary how you could use real terms in jest, when you had established a credible disguise.

'Oh, I say. I'm sorry.' For once Alan's smile gave way to disappointment. Winifred's eye caught Angela's, and stayed there. She said:

'What a pity for us.'

'It's nice of you to put it that way. I'd have liked . . .'

'Perhaps you'll be back before you leave for home?' Winifred suggested.

'I'm not sure . . .'

'Time won't let us,' said Gerald. 'We'll have to carry on back to England.'

'And where are you going from here, exactly?' asked Winifred. She was wearing a bright green bikini, and looked more attractive than Angela had yet seen her. Her body was still an overall shade of cream.

'Uncle Mac wants to look at old Provence,' said Angela, the restored trouper instinct wanting to show M that she could tackle key questions. Careful, though. 'So—we'll be looking at old Provence. Oh, we want to. We were thinking of moving on shortly, and Uncle Mac has only brought us to the boil.'

'I say, yours is a short stay,' said Alan, smiling brightly at M.

'I only came to try and get the family to join me,' said M, 'I'm gratified that I succeeded so easily.'

'We aren't!' said Winifred. 'I'm really sorry you're going.' Angela was surprised. But Winifred's voice had a flatness which seemed to take the pleasurable impact out of any agreeable thing she said. 'Will you be leaving early?'

'Not too early, please,' murmured Caroline, and M said he would try to get them moving by eight o'clock, because cars in hot weather were to be avoided.

'So you won't keep on the move?' This from Alan. He caught Angela's eye and grinned cheerfully.

'Oh, we probably will, away from the coast,' said Father, 'it won't be so hot.'

'I'll just do what I'm told,' giggled Caroline, but reflecting on the truth of her observation. The stage after Cannes she had never been able to foresee and was no nearer to it now.

'Come and have a drink with us tonight at the hotel, do!' cooed Mother to Winifred and Alan. The invitation was as much a dismissal of them for the present as a request for their company in the future. Even Alan got to his feet. As he and Winifred moved away M turned his head, where it lay back still against the chair, and said musingly:

'A pleasant pair.'

'Oh, they're all right,' said Caroline, 'but he's a bit of a silly ass, and she'll dominate him. I wonder why she wants to marry him?'

'Hidden depths,' said Gerald. 'You really shouldn't be so intolerant, sis. If we all wanted the same thing there'd be the most awful queues.' He turned to Uncle Mac. 'Sis and I want to go up Le Suquet this afternoon.' Angela looked in gratitude at his beautiful profile raised in question. 'We've been—waiting for the wind to drop. Sis is awfully keen, and I'd like to go, too. I hope nobody has any other ideas for us this afternoon.'

'I'm sure neither Mabel nor Bruce, and least of all your Uncle Mac, would put anything in the way of that, Peter.' M beamed from nephew to niece.

Mother said, dismissively:

'Yes, of course,' and turned to Father, who was looking pensively out to sea. 'Penny for them!' said Mother, rumpling his hair. Angela felt that Mother now sported the liveliest spirits of them all. Father gave a quick glance and smile towards her, but absently, and turned back to the sea. What did they do at night time? Angela remembered the neatly made beds, side by side. Perhaps they would fall in love with each other and turn the charade into reality, as people seemed to do in the film world. Although there was, as yet, no feel of it in the air. Unless, of course, they had in 'real life' been married to each other for years. There was no reason why she shouldn't believe this, but she didn't.

They had lunch in the hotel, as the men had got so thoroughly out of the beach lunch routine, and Uncle Mac turned it into a festivity. He did most of the talking, telling them anecdotes of his experiences on his way down in the car, and of experiences in France in the past. Mr Bates and Mr Gunter stopped by the table for a word on their way out. Uncle Mac knew them of old, because they had once done a small conversion job on his outhouses. He asked them how they were going to spend the afternoon and when Mr Bates said, 'Exploring' he told them that Peter and Caroline were going to do that too, specifically on Le Suquet.

'Be on your way if you wish,' said M expansively to Caroline and Peter, lighting a cigar after giving one to Father. 'I'm not inclined to hurry.'

'We'll go to the shops when you get back,' said Mother to Caroline, 'for the last time. But not before five.'

So Angela went upstairs in the company of Gerald, Gypsy and Joe, who saw her inside her room.

'What are you laughing at?' Gerald asked her, as Joe and Gypsy withdrew their heads, satisfied, from the quiet interior of Angela's room and went warily into their own.

'I was thinking of *A Midsummer Night's Dream*. In the drama of Pyramus and Thisbe. You know, where someone— Snout, I think—plays the part of Wall. You and Mr Bates—and Mr Gunter—are the men who play my walls—suddenly revealed out of costume.'

But that wasn't true, really. The truth was more like that horror story, where the confident child pulls the mask from her father's face, and finds that the face underneath is still a stranger, and goes mad.

But she was at last on the way to Le Suquet, and it was good to be strolling along the Croisette again, among slow-moving people. The town was quiet, still in the grip of the Gallic lunch hour.

It was very warm, the sun high above their heads. Angela put on her straw coolie hat and knotted her cardigan round her waist rather than carry it—there was already a narrow glistening pool in the crook of her arm. Once or twice on their way west they crossed the road and moved along under the protection of shop and restaurant blinds. Le Suquet beckoned them, hazy-edged in the heat, standing firm between Angela and the unknown dangerous tomorrow.

'Thanks for aiding and abetting me in this.' She took Gerald's hand for a moment, and received an answering squeeze.

'I want to go there, too.'

'Not so much, though, you can take it or leave it.'

'So can you.'

'Only as one can take anything if one has no alternative. I'd have been absurdly disappointed.'

The packed mass of small boats in the old harbour was as still as the old buildings at the foot of the hill. A fat slow dog toiled its way across the Quai St Pierre. As they set foot on the slope Gerald said:

'There's quite a lot of interest up there. Several buildings.'

'Yes. I suppose so. I just saw it as one. Sort of set piece.'

'The clock tower belongs to the sixteenth-century church of Notre Dame de l'Espérance. Isn't it a beautiful name?'

'Oh, yes!'

This was just the sort of conversation she had dreamed of with Gerald, and the setting for it was beyond her wildest dreams. Already, to her left, she could look down on the Croisette and the shore, on the pale coast of Iles de Lérins. In front of her, on the first sharp bend, was a large dilapidated square house in ochre stucco. Parallel, above them, small gardens edged the old wall, heralded by their boundary trees. Only the romantic absorption was missing. The centre of the picture was Le Suquet. And she was not the suppliant of her daydreams.

'Notre Dame de l'Espérance,' repeated Angela, stopping for breath and to mark their position. 'French is a language for prayer—supplication. *"Mère de Dieu"*—is that right?—*"priez pour nous"*. You're not a Catholic?'

'No.' It was only when he had answered that she realised how quietly and smoothly they had both slipped out of their roles. She knew that Peter was Church of England.

'Nor me. But how much more natural—it seems here than the Protestant Church! What else is on top of the hill? And how do you know what there is?'

'I've been reading about it. As you might have done. It makes it more interesting.'

'I know.' Angela would undoubtedly have read about it. Caroline was a bit slap happy. She began to walk on. 'I've nearly finished *Wives and Daughters*. I don't think I've ever been so grateful for a book.'

'Good.'

She was a suppliant in a way, after all. She said humbly: 'Tell me more about the buildings on the top of the hill.'

The bay, which was now on their right, was dropping more and more steeply away. Old men and women sat on the seats beside the narrow pieces of garden which edged the road. The sun commanded a sort of overall quiet, so that Angela and Gerald spoke to each other only just above a whisper.

'The low building with turrets at right angles to the church, that's the chapel of St Anne. Romanesque. We can't go in these days, alas. The church tower isn't the tower of Le Suquet, you know'—when they were two people exchanging information and views they didn't use names, because those available were inappropriate—

238

'that title belongs to the old watchtower in the centre. It was built by the monks of the Islands in the Middle Ages.'

'It's so plain.'

'It's the summit of the hill, despite showy Notre Dame. Two little windows like two little buttons, one above the other.'

'Is this observation, or the book?'

'Observation, that bit.' Well, tomorrow would no doubt make Angela wake up and start taking notice again. 'There's a museum round the tower and the chapel. Antiquities of Egypt, Phoenicia, Greece and Rome. That's the book.'

'I don't think I shall want to go into a museum. Not on my first visit.'

'That suits me.'

They rounded the last bend. At the top of some wide shallow steps the tower of Notre Dame de l'Espérance was cut at its base by a narrow vaulted gateway. Into the Square. Old walls, old trees and plants. The town and the bay revealed in sweeping unimpeded view.

'Here and on the site of St Anne'— Gerald nodded at the low serrated wall ahead of them—'the Abbés of the Lérins must have stood looking at their Islands. St Honorat himself perhaps. While they waited for their boat and a following wind.'

The church, inside, had a gothic up-
ward pull, despite its date. Above the high
altar the Statue of Notre Dame de
l'Espérance shone faintly in the gloom.
The feet of the worshippers shuffled behind them, positioning their owners for
genuflection.

'She has performed miracles,' said
Gerald into Angela's ear, 'she is the object
of pilgrimage.'

They wandered back into the Square. A
liner was breasting the horizon. Somewhere a pigeon was cooing.

'The monks of the Islands, they had
authority over Cannes,' said Gerald, 'that
is, over this old town. They built the
tower—long after St Honorat was dead
and sanctified.'

And long after tomorrow, and after
Angela's morrow of tomorrow, it would
be standing there. She faced the sea and
breathed deeply, feeling comforted.

'Have you really never been here before?'

This could not possibly be a question
for Peter, about whose activities she knew
everything. While she waited she watched
the sea and the island shores behind
Gerald's profile, as ethereally expressionless as the voice of a choirboy. Eventually
he turned to her.

'I have been here before.'

She would let it go at that. 'Then you have been very restrained, postponing a further visit until the very latest moment.'

'You don't know,' said Gerald, 'what Father and I do in the mornings.'

'Ah, no!' So many things she didn't know. She heard her voice forlorn as she went on. 'I'm always making arrogant assumptions.'

He took her hand. 'I don't think so. You're just keen. And brave. And very young.'

'I hope I shan't have to be brave.'

They strolled back hand in hand through the arch of Notre Dame. Angela thought that by tacit consent they had at least temporarily outpaced Caroline and Peter.

Gerald turned to her outside the gates of the Museum.

'You're certain?'

'Yes, I'm certain. You see, I shall come again. I shall buy a house. My father is very, very rich.'

They descended the hill beyond Notre Dame de l'Espérance. The wide shallow steps were tufted with weeds and shone beige and white. On their right was a row of narrow dilapidated houses—pink, ochre, white. Small iron balconies jutted at various levels, shutters were barely ajar.

The balconies were stuffed with drying clothes and with plants whose tendrils trailed down the dingy colour wash. A cage bird shrilled under an overhanging roof. The sun filled the quiet space, dazzling eye and ear. Whenever they stood still, they entered a profound silence.

Opposite the houses were two rosy brick gate posts, topped with flower-filled urns.

'Come in here.'

The iron gate yielded easily, and they were in a garden, a maze of palms and pines and clipped yew hedges and tiny tortuous pebble paths, bounded on the left by the long wall of Le Suquet, plants and flowers protruding from among its stones. They sat down on a stone seat. There was no sound at all, beyond the intermittent frantic singing of the caged bird.

'I should like a house here,' said Angela, 'I truly should.'

Gerald smiled at her. 'You don't look very happy at the happy prospect. You look positively tortured.'

'Do I?' She had to laugh. 'It's funny, beauty and harmony tend to impose a sort of weight on me. It's as if—I want to absorb them, then express them. And my capacities fall short of both.'

'So do all our capacities. And a lot of people don't even have them—capacities, I mean.'

'And I should be comforted by that thought?'

'Well, yes.'

Angela looked round the garden, trying to stamp it on her mind's eye, trying, and failing, to keep other thoughts at bay.

'Gerald, do you think of your family?'

'Yes. Oh, yes.' He wasn't looking at her. His voice and face were expressionless. She might as well not have asked.

'Gerald, why are we moving on if we're safe here? I mean—we're either safe or we're not. There can't be any half way on that. We've either escaped them—or we haven't.'

The canary, or whatever it was, was getting frantic.

'Moving on is part of our brief.' He was staring into space, frowning. 'It's what the Thompsons have undertaken to do. It's the first step on the road home. We must look at it like that. We must trust the people who are protecting us.'

'I try to. I just have a bad feeling . . .'

He turned to look at her then, bleak-faced. 'Certainly the danger will not be over until . . .'

'Until they catch those men?'

'Yes. Until then.'

Those men who killed other men. How many were there? How powerful? There was nothing in the world to keep them from entering even this magic garden.

'We don't know much, do we? We're permanently in the dark.'

'Oh, Angela!'

It was almost a cry, and she took his hand, trying to look into his face, but he kept it turned away. She held on to his limp hand. Both of them sat motionless. The canary had fallen silent.

Notre Dame de l'Espérance struck four o'clock. As if it was a signal, Gerald's hand came to life in hers, twisted round, pulled her to her feet. She looked at him anxiously as she got up, but he was smiling.

'This spot is probably the best bit of it for me,' said Gerald, 'but there's more.'

They wandered about, peering down over stone walls into small lush gardens deep in surrounding cypresses, blobbed with the brilliantly clashing reds of bougainvillaea and oleander. Some of the gardens were so sunk and sheltered that they were already half into shadow. Beyond them, always, were huddled corrugated roofs in bright orange, following the slopes of the hill.

Angela said at last:

'I'll be late for Mother.'

'To hell with Mother!'

Did Gerald say that? His expression, as Angela looked at him quickly, bore no trace of it.

They climbed again, slowly, towards the summit of the hill. In a curve of the steps was a white madonna and child in a white niche.

'That's how religion should be, if it's to be at all,' said Gerald. 'Part of everyday life. The people of Le Suquet will make obeisance to the Mother of God, small public acknowledgement of their adoration, while barely interrupting the joke they're telling their companions. It isn't disrespect, it's the right sort of familiarity.'

'I'm so far from it.'

Gerald gave a brief, rather unpleasant laugh, then took her hand. 'I want to show you a bit of small-scale townscape.'

Beyond the Musée, on the sea side of Le Suquet, the road was lined with terraces of narrow, shabbily colour-washed houses, broken occasionally by stretches of wall which here and there, if they were low or had ill-fitting doors, revealed

245

secluded gardens stretching down the hill. The road circled out of sight, again and again. The first time Angela said she must see round the next corner, Gerald laughed, agreeably this time, in satisfaction. The fourth time he said:

'Aren't you too hot and tired yet?'

She said in surprise:

'I hadn't thought of it. I'm both, I suppose. But you've got to keep chasing it, whatever it is. Isn't that why you brought me here?'

'Of course.'

'Round the next bend might be the answer to it all!'

Round the next bend there was Gypsy, as suddenly as there was a renewed vista of narrow curving street. He was strolling towards them and they saw one another only a moment before there would have been a collision. It took a few minutes for Angela's agitation to become pleasurable. Gypsy didn't go with Le Suquet, or with the mood Le Suquet had induced in her—a mood much older than anything Caroline had taught her, and one which had been rare and precious since childhood.

'Well, well,' said Gypsy.

Angela thought ill temper came and went in Gerald's face, but he turned and fell into step beside Gypsy. The two men made room for Angela between them. As always, she felt she was bridging two worlds.

'We'll go back the other way,' said Gerald.

They came down to the quay via the steep narrow street that sweeps round the inland curve of the hill and is lined with tiny crowded dusty shops and small craft enterprises. In the dark interiors all the metal wares seemed tarnished, all the paper wares curled and yellow. There were mixtures of old books and old silver and seaside rubbish and plastic flowers. In the dark workshops they could see very little, merely hear the small machine noises. Rows of shoes stood outside the shops, sometimes rows of dresses or old books. Because her mood demanded it, Angela bought each of them a doughnut, which they ate as they walked, leaping regularly out of the way of the ubiquitous cars.

'They shouldn't allow cars here!'

'Issues are never as simple as they seem to the young and naïve. It's probably the only access to the streets at the back.'

'I hate you Peter, and if Mr Bates wasn't with us, I'd show you.'

They walked back along the Croisette, not talking much but remaining now strictly in character. Mother was sitting on the hotel terrace, alone at a table under a tree, reading a magazine and waiting for her daughter. They were late, but she was smiling.

'We bumped into Mr Bates!'

'So I see.'

'Sorry we're late.'

'Go and have a cool wash,' said Mother generously, 'change your shoes or something, put your feet up for five minutes. Peter and Mr Bates will keep me company.'

Angela was certain that the smiled remark, accompanied by faintly coquettish glances at Gerald and Gypsy, was an order. As she crossed the threshold of the hotel she looked back to see both men sitting down in unison one each side of Mother. No wonder they had so cheerfully let her and Gerald go off walking on their own, Gypsy had been deputed to keep an eye on them. He must have been in sight of them the whole time they had been wrapped in their enchanted solitude on the hill, and had 'met' them at the time he decided upon. No doubt Joe, too, had been within call. It was ungrateful of her to feel irritated before she felt reassured.

Over *café liègeois* with Mother, Angela talked more than usual, unable to keep to herself the impact of Le Suquet, not really needing a response and not getting it beyond smiles and murmurs, but sorting out her impressions as she chatted on. Paramount was a small but real sense of achievement, the sort of feeling she had had on discovering she had committed to memory enough Shakespeare to compensate for sleepless nights. Now, she had wrested from her dangerous situation a memory which she could enjoy into the future—a pinnacle, after all, rising from her Mediterranean afternoons. The glow of the achievement almost masked the other noticeable sensation. What was it? A sort of sadness, a regret . . . Her original dream that she and Gerald would have things in common, would see them the same way, against an exotic background, it had come true. But in the end, somehow, she had been unable to do anything about it.

I know a lady in Venice . . .

But it was nothing like so simple as that.

'I've enjoyed this part of the holiday so much, Mother,' ventured Angela, as Mother picked up her bag and the pastel chiffon scarf which always floated from it, or from her hand. Mother never said anything about moving on, she just collected her belongings, and then Angela found herself on her feet, helping Mother out of her chair.

'So have I, dear.' Mother permitted the rare occurrence of meeting Angela's eye, and smiling. She smiled again, with the suspicion of a wink, later in the rue d'Antibes, when she bought a frothy lace handkerchief bearing the initial 'C', and handed it to Angela.

'A present from Cannes,' said Mother.

Alan and Winifred came promptly as invited on to the terrace before dinner, and Winifred took Alan away at the appropriate time. Both of them seemed regretful that the Thompsons were leaving, but their regret stopped short of a request for the Thompson address, which was a relief, although this eventuality had been covered in Gypsy's lessons.

Dinner in the hotel, with M present, was a much longer and more talkative process than it normally was. But for Angela, now, the visit to the seaside was over. Alone in her room as soon as possible, she was eager to start packing so that she could no longer delude herself that this apparently safe, comfortable, familiar pattern of life was going to continue . . .

The three matching suitcases were in a pyramid on top of the wardrobe. She could just reach up and grip the jutting edge of the large one at the bottom of the pile, pull it slowly and carefully towards her. But the top cases began to slide along and bring the balance down too rapidly for her to control it, and although she caught the largest case on both her hands and held it, the other two bounced down on to the floor with two separate crashes into the silence, right outside the door that led to Gypsy's room.

He was there instantly, with his gun. Angela just had time to pull the tumbled suitcases out of his path. They looked at each other, and Gypsy put the gun slowly away inside his jacket.

'I'm sorry,' said Angela, 'the cases fell off the wardrobe. I was too anxious to get them down.' She was out of breath.

Gypsy grinned. 'Too anxious to get moving, doll?'

'Oh, no, Gypsy, I don't want to move. I'm—frightened of moving. But when I've got to go anywhere—I like to get on with it.'

'Yeah, I know.'

He picked the largest suitcase off the floor and put it on the luggage rack. Put the other cases on the bed.

'Thanks, Gypsy.'

She was standing beside him. With the merest movement she could touch him.

'Gypsy . . .'

He turned, in his abrupt way, to face her, grasping her upper arms firmly in his hands.

'You're all right, doll!'

It was a command. She whispered despairingly, again:

'Gypsy . . .' and he stared at her severely and she shuffled her feet so that she was close to him, and instantly his arms were tightly round her, his lips pressing hers, parting them, his hands learning the shape of her body. There was a moment when she might have recoiled from the shock of his strength and energy to such a purpose, but another sensation was stronger and she began to respond.

She wasn't thinking. She wasn't in her usual way working out what she was doing, or would do, or why. She just wanted to be near Gypsy, as near as possible. It seemed she had wanted that for a long time.

'No, doll!'

Gypsy staggered back, and was glaring at her. His hair where she had pulled it was on his forehead. His mouth looked swollen, like hers felt. She put her hands out.

'Gypsy!'

He lifted his arms in a helpless gesture, and let them fall to his sides. They looked at one another. A sense of shame began to ooze into Angela, clammy and uncomfortable.

Gypsy told her to sit down, and took the other chair. He sat leaning forward, his hands dangling between his knees, as he had sat so often and looked at her, through a whole range of facial expressions. Now he had none. Angela thought he was puzzled. She heard herself say:

'I'm sorry.'

'No!' He lit a cigarette. Angela found herself taking the ashtray off her bedside table and putting it on the arm of his chair. He drew in smoke. He said gently:

'This won't do, doll, you know that.' Angela was silent, and he said, roughly, 'You know. Christ, you know!'

'Yes,' she mumbled.

'I'm here to look after you. And if I was to—that would be the end of me, doll!'

'Oh, Gypsy!'

'Keep your voice down. No damage done. But none to be done. Doll, what do you take me for?'

She thought he was really upset, horrified of possibilities. She said again,

'I'm sorry.'

Perhaps it was, anyway, that even Caroline had had enough. She didn't know, although she would try to find out—if she could penetrate the extraordinary brilliance which already encircled the incident in her memory.

Gypsy ground his cigarette out and got up, pulling her with him by the shoulders. He kissed her forehead. 'Goodnight, doll, sweet dreams.'

She was too tired, too content with what had happened, to be really disappointed.

'I'll never forget you, Gypsy.'

His golden grin flashed out and Angela managed an uncertain smile. He said:

'Pack those bags now, and be ready by eight in the morning.'

'Gypsy . . . do you believe that I don't usually behave—like this? I've never behaved like this, Gypsy.'

He put his hand on her hair. 'Doll—I can guess that! And I've never received such a compliment. Never in my long hard life!'

'Gypsy!'

She held out her arms and there was a moment when everything in the world could have happened. She knew it then, and knew it ever afterwards. A light of joy and amazement leapt into Gypsy's eyes.

But he turned away. 'You do that job

now, doll,' he said, scrubbing his dead cigarette end about in the ash tray, 'and then get some sleep. And don't worry, it may never happen.'

He gave the bitter laugh she had heard once before, and went back through the connecting door without looking at her again. She heard the key turn.

'I know,' she said to the door, 'that's the trouble.'

In the morning she and Mother, Father and Peter and Uncle Mac left Cannes at eight-thirty, without seeing Mr Gunter or Mr Bates to say goodbye.

—— CHAPTER 11 ——————

Tuesday, 1st July
Pen to paper. A strange sensation. I've never gone so long without writing—anything, not a letter, not even a post-card. Nothing. Oh, except 'Caroline Thompson' I suppose, I've written that. Gypsy told me in the flat that I mustn't write anything when we went to France, and I promised. And I didn't really miss it, not even my diary. Until we arrived here. I missed it right away, then. And I

told Gerald, and then Gypsy gave me this book and this pen and said I could write if I wanted something to do—'While you're waiting.' He said 'While you're waiting'—I could write anything because this house was—safe. That was the word he used, 'safe'. It feels like a prison.

Gerald, my fellow-prisoner, has seen to it all along that I have the things that are vital to me: reading, writing, Le Suquet. I think about Le Suquet. We've only been here three days, less than that, but it's a long, long time ago. I think about Gerald too. I love Gerald, with a true love.

But I shouldn't have to think about Gerald, I should be with him. Why aren't I with him? There aren't any training sessions, any more. Why can't I be with him? Now.

I think I was afraid of coming here because I knew somehow that everything would change, break up. I was right. When I nearly destroyed the family in Cannes it was dreadful—hearing Father call me 'the girl'. But somehow, all of a sudden, it doesn't matter any more. I'm glad I feel like this, because I can see that the family isn't—what it was. Well—why bother when there's nobody to play up to, nobody to convince any more? If life's going to be like it has been since we arrived here, we shan't be seeing people, going out and about, except for air and exercise. Prisoners have exercise time, half an hour in the open air. That's what my walks feel like with Gerald and Gypsy and Joe. Gypsy keeps looking at his watch. Half an hour in the morning, half an hour after tea.

The afternoons are the worst. I have to surmount the afternoons. It's mid afternoon now.

From my window I look down on the Place. This is a funny old house, tall and thin. It's semi-detached from the village school. The children make a terrible noise when they come out for their morning break, screaming and shouting—I could hardly believe it when I looked out and there were only a dozen of them. I have a dreadful feeling, that if we're here for long, like this, I may scream and shout too when I'm let out to walk.

When I came up here after lunch, a bus was dropping off a party of tourists. The bus is still there, the tourists haven't reappeared. The old man's dog has just lifted its leg against one of the wheels.

I have a marvellous view from my window. Not just the Place. I'm on the top floor. The house has four floors, with only a room or two on each—like the houses on Le Suquet. That day on Le

Suquet was the last day of peace, some-how. Although of course I didn't know it at the time. I thought I was worried, then. It's funny. The Place is surrounded by enormous plane trees and a low wall on one side. The plane trees cover the ground with shadows. I can see over the wall, on to countryside that stretches out of sight. It's like those backgrounds you glimpse in renaissance paintings—the bits of plain and river and hill which are more exciting (to me) than all the madonnas in the fore-ground. Today it's misty. I can only guess at it really. It's been misty since we ar-rived. Perhaps it will be clearer tomorrow. A reason for jumping out of bed in the morning.

The whole village is an Ancient Monu-ment. *'Stoppé'*, as the French amusingly put it. It has entrances in the ancient walls. The buildings are all lovely and old and shabby and some of the streets are so narrow you could almost shake hands across them, and terribly steep. Then you suddenly come out into a great flat open space—like our Place, and the Place de l'Eglise. The church is marvellous—like the chapel of St Anne on Le Suquet, only you can go in here, of course, and they let Gerald and me go in for a few moments last evening. Very dark rich windows, predominant blue and purple light. Un-adorned interior. The stone of these romanesque churches looks like terrine.

Now I've run out of that bit of steam I realise I was Making an Effort. I'm frightened. I keep thinking about those men after the Bella Ball. I dream of blood. Horrible. Why have we holed up here? Because we *have* holed up, I feel it. We've dug ourselves in. But the men either know we're here, or they don't. I don't understand. But then they probably wouldn't have told us the full truth—Special Branch, I mean. Why should they? If the family's going to be less important now, perhaps Gerald and I can talk to each other properly. If there's ever the opportunity. Why can't we be together? Even when we played Scrabble last night, Joe was there.

There's a Sid here, French version. I wonder how secret *his* service is? As soon as we arrived here, things were different. The same people had lunch as had had dinner together in Cannes the night before, but it was different. Of course, Mr Bates and Mr Gunter being here with the Thompsons didn't fit. Oh, yes, Joe and Gypsy arrived soon after we did. I wasn't really surprised.

If I don't call her Mother, and him Father, what do I call them?

The village is out of this world. The whole thing seems like a growth of the rock. And on the other side, if you look over the wall of the Place de l'Eglise, you can see for miles and miles over vineyard country to distant hills and a small blue gap which Gerald said was the sea. Every little wedge of land seems to be cultivated.

We came straight here. A couple of hours. No hesitation, everything arranged and expected.

It's half past four. There's a sitting-room here, on the ground floor. We eat at one end of it, and Gerald and I play Scrabble there in the evening. I suppose I could go downstairs but Mother said: 'Have a rest.' Like she said yesterday, and the day before. She hasn't said: 'Stay in your room until somebody tells you to come out of it,' and the door isn't locked (oh, God, of course not, what's the matter with me?). But I think I'll wait till I'm called.

The house is very quiet. The school's closed for the day. The old man is still in the Place, with his old dog. They're looking over the wall. The old man is, I mean. The dog's sniffing about. I hope we can go for a walk later on. We *must* go. I wonder if M will be back for dinner, he

260

wasn't here at lunchtime. These things aren't worth writing down, but I keep getting on tenterhooks. I don't know why, I don't think the granite-faced men are suddenly going to break into the house. But I can't relax. Somehow I don't feel part of a team any more. I feel on my own. I should like someone to reassure me.

Things must have gone well up to now. I tell myself that we're just waiting here until all the men are caught, then going home. I want to ask M about Mummy and Daddy, but I can't. Caroline can't. And we're still the Thompsons, if we're anything. But I don't believe in Caroline any more.

I don't know why I feel so agitated. I think it's because suddenly I'm living with strangers. That's ridiculous, I know I always was, but in Cannes the family felt real—it's absurd, but it did. If Gerald could be with me it would be different. But I don't think they're going to let us be together again.

Why not? Why on earth not? What difference would it make?

I must stop thinking like this, it doesn't get anywhere, except it makes me more agitated. They know what they're doing. Perhaps writing isn't such a good idea, it makes me think too much. Reading helps me not to think. I've got Daudet's *Petit Chose* and Sagan's *Une Certaine Sourire* and I haven't quite finished *Wives and Daughters*.

My hand's aching, agony, I'm not used to writing! The view over the Place wall is getting hazier and hazier. The coach has taken the tourists away.

I'm going to read.

Wednesday, 2nd July

I've just burned my finger. That was because I was burning some paper. I wanted to write down about the last night in Cannes, and what I've felt, so last night I did. And then just now I burned it. It's burned to ashes, and it's in the waste-paper basket. I didn't mind burning it in the end, it was the writing it that mattered. Not that it was anything. But when I get home I shall be quite, quite different when I meet men. I know now how you can want it to happen.

If I get home.

I want to go home. So badly I keep imagining myself creeping downstairs when we've gone to bed, negotiating the door (it has a big bolt on it but of course I don't know how stiff it is), then running and running towards the nearest gate and out of the village. But there's a long winding road down to the valley and then miles of countryside. I am a prisoner, I really am. Sometimes I think of going and hiding on one of those coaches, there always seems to be one on the Place, and leaving with the tourists.

But that's crazy, I'm safe here, that's why I'm here, that's why they sent me to France, to be safe. It's only that I miss Mummy and Daddy so much.

I coincided with M in the hall this morning. I mumbled to him about 'everyone being all right—*you* know'—fatuous and feeble—and he was *impatient* for a moment, he said, 'Yes, yes!', and then he looked at me—and then I saw him sort of settle down into himself again, and he said, 'I can assure you, my dear' (this saves either Angela or Caroline, of course), 'that all is well in the direction where your—ah—maximum anxieties lie,' or something like that. But I had the feeling he was rattled, that he had had to make an effort to be like he always used to be, and I've got that sort of feeling about everyone.

It's difficult to pin it down. Joe doesn't change, obviously, because with Joe there's nothing to change. Nor Father much, just that he doesn't have those expansive moods any more. M usually rallies Mother with a bit of chat—about the village or France generally or something impersonal but then she falls back into a sort of gloom, she looks worried and then she hides it and that blank look comes over her face and then it slips again. She and Gerald don't entertain one another any more. Gerald looks so worried, I think he feels like I do, but there's no chance to ask him. Gypsy—he doesn't tease me now or look at me, he doesn't laugh, he's tense.

We don't talk Thompson any more, and we don't talk the real situation. I can't see any reason, now, why we don't, why we can't talk about the one thing that's in all our minds, but we don't, and somehow I can't be the one to break the ice.

So now we're people without any names, real, or unreal. If I want to ask Mother something I wait until I catch her eye, and then I say 'you'. All our bits of conversation are either practical—'There isn't any salt in this damn thing—*René!*'—or general—about the village, or news in the papers, etcetera. It's a funny thing how habits, even rules, seem to develop without ever being decided in words. Yet I'm sure somehow that there are lots of words—fateful words—being spoken behind all these walls and doors (I don't even know which room is whose, or who's with whom, if any of them are), but of course I don't hear any of them. I don't even know the name of the village!

It's afternoon again. Hateful afternoon. I lay down on the bed when I came up after lunch and even went to sleep for half an hour, but I felt so awful when I woke up that I got up and burned those pages because I wanted something to do. I really did burn my right index finger, the skin's blistering.

There's a bit of a wind today, and the plane tree shadows are flickering on the yellow dust of the Place. That sounds like the first line of a novel. I might write a novel one day. I've got more to say now than I had a few weeks ago. There's a coach there again. Cars aren't allowed to park in the Place, only coaches. That isn't as illogical as it sounds, because there only ever seems to be one coach at a time.

The view is a bit clearer today. I think I can see water gleaming, and vineyards and olives into the distance.

The bathroom is next to my room. It has such a funny old bath—on two levels like a chair—the sitting part is even moulded to your BTM. Your shoulders get cold. But even in the summer this house is cold. No sun ever gets into it. It's such a relief to step into the Place and feel the sudden sun. I'm really cold in here, although I can see the brilliance and imagine the heat outside. If only there was a garden. If I could just lie in the sun, the time would pass, and I'd feel better. Actually, there is a garden, which makes it worse, like a form of torture: there's a window in the sitting-room (where the sun comes a few feet into the room in the morning) with a window seat which looks out on a little gravelly garden, which I think belongs to the house opposite. Nobody uses it! I wish I could. I wish it so much, I feel like Alice peering into the beautiful garden she was too big to enter. I am too—ignorant. Well, that's how I feel. I sit on the window seat after breakfast, feeling the warmth. Gerald and Joe and Gypsy and I have breakfast, but afterwards they all disappear and I sit on the window seat on my own. Where do they all go, especially Gerald? Where is Gerald now? Why can't we be together? We were together in Cannes—but not all that much, I suppose, now I think about it. Does he sit in his room and write and read and think? I don't think he is well, he is very pale. Mother and Father don't appear for breakfast. Or M.

I said the 'bathroom' just now, but it can't be the only one. I've never met anyone coming or going. There's only one other room on this floor. I tried the door once and it was locked. I don't even know if anyone uses it. Sometimes at night I've thought I've heard sounds on the landing. Gypsy has never been up to my room.

How slowly the time goes. And then the walks are over before I know. I should like to stop outside one of the little bars for a drink in the sun, but we never do.

We must be in danger.

I can never talk to Gerald. I tried to ask him while we were playing Scrabble last night what he does, but Joe was there. Well, I did ask him and it's ridiculous, no one has said I mustn't, but I was all nervous and giggly, like I used to be with him at the beginning, and he just said, 'There isn't much choice, is there?' and then I *did* say, 'But why can't we be together more?' and he looked at me with that sudden sad look he's given me only a few times ever, but quite shattering, and said, 'Remember we're with people who know exactly what they're doing', and I felt a bit better.

But not for long, although I have to remember that Gypsy and Joe stick with us to protect us, not to keep us prisoners.

I've just stopped off to have a cry, and I feel better. Well, less bothered. Why am

I so bothered? Why do I keep feeling I can't and mustn't do things when no one's actually told me?

This seems to be the laziest life in the world, but I think we're all on edge, pumping out gallons of adrenalin and nervous energy.

I had an awful dream last night that I would go on like this for ever, seeing the sun and not feeling it, not having a name or knowing why anything was happening, toiling up and down stairs from one anonymous place to another, getting little false hopes of asking questions next time I see 'Them' but always being disappointed, seeing the seasons change from this window, piling up notebooks, watching the pigeons and the tourists and the children.

But it isn't the same, because the people are changing. Making less and less effort. Getting more and more tense. We're coming near to something. I hope it's only the fact of going home. I wish René would come and tell me tea's ready. The afternoons are the worst.

The tourists are tottering back to the bus. Always the dullest people come out of long distance buses. A lot of pink frocks of different shades among the women. All awful. One man in braces. Must be

English. They look hot and tired. I have goosefleshy arms, it's ridiculous.

This morning we went into one of the few shops and I bought some faience, with the francs I won at the Casino. A green and white vase and a plate with lovely pierced edge. I forgot things, just for a moment, while I looked round the shop. Will I ever hand them over to Mummy?

My heart's pounding. It's absurd, but I wish somebody would reassure me.

The coach is driving off. I wish I was hiding under one of the seats. I'd rather die with Mummy and Daddy than away from them.

That's ridiculous. I'm going to read.

Thursday, 3rd July
'*Mère de Dieu, priez pour nous*'. I keep finding that in my mind, saying it over and over. On Le Suquet it caught my imagination, I thought of persecuted Catholics on their knees in hostile places of history, whispering '*Mère de Dieu, priez pour moi*'. Now, I don't know if I'm just remembering it because it's haunting, like the line of a song, or whether I'm saying it for real. Asking for something. Protection, if anything. But I've got it already. What's the matter with me? I feel permanently in the dark.

You wouldn't think it was possible to be in a house with seven other people, and feel so alone. Of course, I suppose there are times when they could most of them be out, and that's something else I wouldn't know, they mightn't use the door on to the Place, there's another door in the wall, at the side, where we came in the first time.

I've nothing to write about. Well, there is something, which I don't want to write about. But I will. Gerald—I'm losing him somehow, they're telling him things they're not telling me. He must be under some sort of pressure I don't know about. Perhaps Special Branch have given him a job. Something dangerous it must be—why else would they keep us apart, and he be so impatient with me? He looks ill, I'm sure now he's under some extra strain, something I don't know about, otherwise we'd be together now, and he'd be making me feel better. I took his hand last night when we were out walking, and he let it stay there.

But he hardly ever looks at me. When we play Scrabble he concentrates on the board and when he laughs at anything I say he laughs sort of carefully and keeps his eyes down. I think they must have let him into a secret they've made him promise not to tell me. A bad secret.

All this means that there must be danger. I try not to think about home, because just round the corner I have fears that I wouldn't be able to bear. I can't ask M any more.

When M is jolly now, I get the feeling it's because he's suddenly remembered that this is his image. Not that I see him much, or Mother and Father. Just at meals, though M isn't here for them all. Mother and Father just eat and look at their plates, and go out.

Breakfast is the best, because that's when the sun comes into the sitting-room window, and I'm so glad to get downstairs, out of this room. It's getting more and more difficult to control my thoughts. Each time the children scream in the Place, I feel more and more like joining in. I'm glad to hear the children, now.

Gerald hardly said a word at breakfast this morning. He looked so pale and worried, I went up to him and kissed his cheek. He turned away from me but he didn't move away. I think he can't look at me because of what he knows, and mustn't tell me. Something dreadful. So that now there's no one to share my ignorance and my terrors. Gerald's terrified, but he knows what about.

I keep thinking it could be Mummy and Daddy, and they'll keep it from me as long as possible. I mustn't think that. I can't.

René is a good cook—unless there's somebody else in the kitchen, and he's just front-of-house man. I've never been in the kitchen here, I just walk up and down the stairs between this room and the sitting-room, past closed doors. All the doors are closed, always. I'm not hungry, these days. No one seems to be hungry. M sometimes tries to rally us to eat more, when he remembers his image, and then he overdoes it, says that the chef will be offended. No one here now is worrying about things like that.

But I wish René would come and tell me tea's ready. I wonder whose house this is. It has quite nice liveable-with French provincial furniture, but no bits and pieces, no clues to anyone who's lived here—or still does. Just efficiency again. I can't imagine it's a house that belongs to SB. They couldn't have permanent places in every remote corner of Europe. But they must have contacts. That's what counts, I suppose. Then you can get any-thing in a hurry, anywhere.

'*Mère de Dieu.*' Thank God we're still going for walks. I said to Gerald last night, loudly, when both Gypsy and Joe were in the room, when I was putting the Scrabble away, I said, 'I'm grateful for these games, almost as grateful as I am for our walks.' Gerald said: 'So you like our walks?' and I said: 'I need them.' And I looked hard at Gypsy and Joe, who were standing by in their usual way. They have this air of looking into space, and Gypsy lolls, but they're both *ready*. Hard to explain, how one can dawdle with intent, but Gypsy does. They didn't look at me when I spoke about the walks but of course they heard. At meals I always make a point of being enthusiastic about them, and retailing what I've seen. It usually falls flat (only M if he's there makes a bit of dialogue out of it) but I'm entertaining myself, if nobody else. Sometimes Gerald looks faintly annoyed, and I remember those early days when he seemed so far out of my reach and sometimes I feel as if I've dreamed everything in between— Caroline queening along the Casino corridors and Gerald and I talking about everything and each caring what the other one thought (I'm sure of it) and the sunshine and the sea and the gaiety of the cafés and that night . . .

I'm not fat any more. Quite lean in fact. I took myself unawares in the long mirror in the bathroom last night. It's covered in speckles like mildew and I couldn't see all that clearly in the gloom anyway—but I'm not fat. I'd have been over the moon at home but now it doesn't mean very much. I've an idea that you never get anything in life at the pitch of your yen for it.

Is there any future ahead of us? I wish René would come. I'm afraid if I go down on my own they may be angry, and so far nobody has been angry. Why do I feel it isn't very far away? Anger, I mean.

There's a bus there again, empty. We met a group of tourists this morning, round a corner. I saw Gypsy's hand fly to his pocket. Everyone's so edgy. One woman was arguing with her husband about a camera setting. She was all steamed up about it. Fancy only having something like that to worry about!

The locals say, 'Bonjour' to us. I think this worries Gypsy and Joe, they want to be anonymous. I know they would rather not take me out. But I must get out. *Mère de Dieu*. Our Father, let them still take me out. Every prisoner is allowed air and exercise.

The cats and dogs are friendly here— with us and with each other. René told me that the cats and dogs of the village are a team. If there are any visiting quadrupeds, they gang up against them! Poor strangers. The shade of doorways and terraces and staircases round the Place, and round the Place de l'Eglise, is full of thin motionless cats. Dogs lie under the tables outside the cafés. I don't suppose we'll ever sit down at one of those, now, it gets more unlikely somehow each day. When we walk we never go outside the old walls, but there's plenty of variety inside. On our evening walk men are playing *boule* in the Place de l'Eglise.

I'm not frightened every single minute, but more and more often. The afternoons are the worst. I'll stop writing now and read until René comes. The tourists have left. I wish I wasn't so cold. I want to feel the sun not just see it. My tan has lost its glow. So has my expression, gone with Caroline. Angela's eyes look back at me from the mirror, not confident any more. But I haven't got any spots, and I haven't used Carys's cream for a while now. Carys! I'd almost forgotten her, she seems so long ago. When I think back to the flat I know I've changed. Inside as well as in looks.

It's as if a spell was cast on me in Cannes, and now it's broken. Just as well, it was a dozy dream. I feel now as if the Thompsons were a family I knew, then lost contact with, to my regret. But well—these things happen. That's how I feel.

I could do with some books to work with, only I don't suppose I could concentrate. I'm too churned up. We're getting nearer and nearer to things now. To what? Why do I say that? I don't know. Dear God, our Father, keep Mummy and Daddy safe. Don't let it be—that.

In an hour's time I shall be in the sun. They wouldn't stop that.

Friday, 4th July
Mother and M have gone. Gone for good. At the end of lunch M made an *announcement*, in his old style. But he called me 'Angela', marking the final breakup of the family. In Cannes I should have been heartbroken, but it was dead anyway. He said something like: 'Mrs—er—Thompson'—only possible name, to me—'and I will now be leaving you, Angela. We are all moving nearer to an—er—return to normality.' (Beam. Beam. Like old times.) 'It is unlikely that we shall meet again. You, too, will be moving shortly on the first stages of your—er—journey home.'

I felt marvellous for a moment, but why do they look so worried? Why do I feel tension all round, see Gypsy and Joe rush their right hands to their pockets whenever we encounter a wretched peasant?

But M has gone, and Mother. I caught her eye as I looked away from M, so I said 'Goodbye', and she said 'Goodbye', with a tired little smile. Then I said, feeling frightfully inadequate, 'Thank you so much.' How ridiculous! But what could I say? It's hardly a situation you could learn how to handle from books on etiquette. Perhaps I owe her my life. She smiled again, just, and went out with M. I'll puzzle over her as long as I live.

So then there were five. How soon is 'shortly'?

Just after M and Mother had gone, there were only Gerald and I in the room. I said to him something about how marvellous it would be to walk with him and play Scrabble with him in safety, in normal life, how I was looking forward to it, and he just gave me that sad look—sadder than ever—and charged out of the room.

It isn't as simple as M says. He doesn't want me to panic so he feeds me guff. But

I would prefer to know the truth. I think Gerald knows it.

Saturday, 5th July

I'm getting that I can't read now. Or write. Only sit and stare out of the window and palpitate. Gerald only played one game with me last night. I tried to ask him to tell me what was wrong but he said 'Nothing' and then said it would all soon be over.

We didn't talk at all at breakfast. Nor lunch time. As we got up from lunch, Gypsy said: 'Upstairs!' as if I was a dog and I said, 'Gerald!' and he said, 'All right, all right,' and, 'That'll do' to Gypsy, and Gypsy shrugged his shoulders. He must be awfully jumpy. Why? Why? I found I was crying and saying, 'As long as you let me come down for a walk. *Please!*' And Gypsy and Gerald looking at each other and Gerald saying, very deliberately as if daring Gypsy: 'Yes, of course, we shall have a walk'. And Gypsy shrugged again and I ran out of the room and up here and cried and cried and felt better, a bit.

But tomorrow and tomorrow and tomorrow.

I can't read or write.

The tourist coach that was here before lunch has gone. It looks so hot, but I'm shivering. Cold inside my body, in my spine. I want to feel the sun, get out of here.

Mère de Dieu, père, fils, priez pour moi.

I suppose I'm awfully *ungrateful*, writing like this. When people are doing so much to protect me. I'll feel better after the walk this evening.

René, please come and tell me it's teatime.

It was strange, how the goose pimples rose on her arms, under the impact of the late afternoon sun. They stood waiting by the door, while Joe locked it. Angela, Gerald and Gypsy. Angela felt a small breeze stir her hair. She shivered, in the welcome heat.

'Cold?' Gerald looked concerned, touched her arm with his own cold hand. His appearance was as immaculate as ever but there was something disordered in his eyes, the way they slid on and off her face.

'It's just all those hours in that cold house.'

'I know.'

She took his hand and walked with him across the Place de l'Ecole. Gypsy and Joe strolled behind them. The breeze must be a wind in the treetops, the shadows of the highest branches of the planes surged so wildly on the yellow grit under her sandals. Angela stopped to shake out some pebbles, releasing Gerald's limp hand and putting hers on his shoulder for balance, and Gypsy and Joe stopped one each side of them.

The countryside below the wall that edged the Place stretched tranquil out of sight, progressively paler and more misty. The far horizon was lost in haze. Water glinted between jigsaw pieces of field, vine and olive. Cars moved in the distance, small and jerky like insects. There was no sound but the sighing of a pigeon.

Angela looked back across the Place, to the shuttered school and her small window. Oh, but she didn't want to go back inside, however safe . . .

'Gerald . . .'

Gypsy and Joe had no visible reaction to this avowal, in the open air, of the disappearance of the Thompson family. Angela laughed—half effort, half hysteria—and Gerald squeezed her hand.

Beyond his perfect profile she saw a tourist bus lumber into the Place. A rather smaller bus than usual, something between a bus and a mini-bus. When it came to a halt the passengers remained seated, and she saw that the courier was addressing them. He must be pointing out the directions in which he was going to take them: she could see the silent movement of his mouth, the heads swivelling about, eyes passing unseeingly over her and her escorts.

The bus wasn't full. Most of the passengers seemed to be men. As Angela, Gerald, Gypsy and Joe walked slowly away from the wall the tourists at last began to descend. Angela smiled to herself, they looked so bored, so uninterested in their surroundings. Another party, wanting to be able to say they had 'done' a Provençal village. Perhaps a youth group—there were no older men or matrons. The young men were rather good-looking . . .

The tourists seemed to be making their way towards the same narrow street which marked the start of Angela and Gerald's regular walk. Gypsy and Joe hung back, to let the party through, but they too paused, talking quietly among themselves, pointing across the Place to the horizon. A thin black cat ran swiftly between them, undeflected by Angela's blandishments. The old man and his dog were standing near the bus and the cat made up briefly to the dog as it went by. The tourists were still standing around.

'Are they going or aren't they?' demanded Gerald pettishly.

'It doesn't matter,' answered Angela, consciously breathing open air.

The black cat returned, still intent on its purposes. With an exclamation of impatience, Gerald stepped forward, pulling Angela with him. Gypsy shrugged. He and Joe followed.

At the same time the tourists began to move towards the mouth of the little street. They arrived there with Angela, Gerald, Gypsy and Joe. Caught up with the tourists, Angela listened, as she always did, for their voices, not this time to confirm her guess as to their nationality and status, but to resolve a total enigma.

But none of them seemed, now, to be speaking. They were all simply moving. Moving relentlessly down the narrow channel with Angela, Gerald, Gypsy and Joe in their midst. Angela caught Gerald's eye and gave him a mock-anguished grimace. She thought he returned it, and then the press of people carried her away from him despite her clutching hand, towards an open door giving on to the narrow street.

She tried to get back towards Gerald, back into the middle of the road, but the pressure of bodies was too strong, she couldn't move against it. It was so strong it was actually carrying her inside, through the doorway. She tried to fight it, but was still carried forward. The faces, now so close to her, were without expression. Still silent. But behind her she heard an oath, in English, and the beginning of a scuffle.

Angela tried to look round but she was right inside the doorway, now, inside the building. The doorway behind her, the means of escape, was full of bodies, but such was the force of another body that it hurled them apart, and stood beside her. It was Gerald. Angela saw that a curl had fallen forward over his eyes, as so long ago after the Bella Ball.

It was dark inside the building. Angela tried to find Gerald's hand. He shouted her name and her response was drowned in the deafening explosion of a shot. Gerald had disappeared. There was another shot. The scuffling behind her was now a fight, with grunting sounds like the sounds she had heard in the darkness after the ball.

There was a third shot, it no longer jarred her, she was used to shots, but this one she felt the draught of past her face. She thought she heard Gypsy's voice. Somebody grabbed her arm and pulled her roughly to the ground. There was another shot. The fight was going on all round her, above her head. She was in a sort of clearing on flagged ground, a stone was hurting her knee. The fight swayed above her, in the clearing with her was Gerald, lying awkwardly on his side, his eyes staring at her unseeingly, blood trickling out of the corner of his mouth.

'*No, Gerald, no!*'

Even in the turmoil, Angela heard her shriek of protest. She put up a sort of prayer for oblivion, which was answered. Something struck her violently on the back of the head.

—— CHAPTER 12 ——

The world was very quiet and calm and white. That was all it was, and yet it was infinite. White everywhere, breathing calm and quiet.

Angela was part of it, breathing gently in time with it. She was nothing but a gently breathing acknowledgement and celebration of this calm white world.

Slowly, very slowly, it closed in. The white world was white walls, an open window with a white curtain blowing. A white cover over the inert lump of her body.

And something else which made her frown like a disappointed child, and become aware of her limbs as she kicked a leg in irritation. Something that was not white, or silent, but kept, very softly, saying:

'Angela. Angela.'

It was the face of Alan Boyce. Whoever Alan Boyce might be. And beside him was Winifred Holland, his fiancée. There was something wrong with them both. Winifred Holland had wet eyes and a trembling mouth. And Alan Boyce . . .

They must be part of a dream, the usual crazy dream where familiar people do absurd and unfamiliar things, change into other people, act out of their characters. She would dismiss them in a new sleep. Sleep . . . It was the only thing you could be sure of . . .

Angela closed her eyes again, and when she opened them years or minutes later, Alan Boyce and Winifred Holland were still there, and they were still wrong.

Angela said wonderingly, to Alan Boyce, 'You haven't got a silly-ass face after all.'

Alan Boyce turned to Winifred. 'What do you think of that?' he asked.

Winifred smiled through what could almost be called her tears.

'It shows you did well.'

Angela saw her press Alan's hand. Their presence no longer annoyed her, although she didn't know why they were there, she didn't know anything about them, much less why she was convinced they had changed. It was pleasant to lie back in peace and comfort, and see what happened. Although somewhere, not very far off, was the possibility of alarm.

Winifred asked her, gently, how she was feeling.

'I feel fine.' How should she feel? But how gentle Winifred was, almost timid in the way she kept half smiling at Angela! Alan Boyce was very determined-looking, handsome and with attractive hands. Funny how she didn't think she remembered his good looks. She remembered his hands, though, they hadn't changed. The alarm started to ring a faint bell.

'Good, good,' said Alan, sounding cautious but encouraging. He smiled firmly at Angela.

'You've changed,' she said.

Again Alan and Winifred exchanged glances.

'Not really,' began Winifred, and Alan said, 'Sh!' sharply, watching Angela, so that Winifred whispered, 'Sorry, Alan,' and sat back in her chair.

How did she know they had changed when she didn't know who they were?

Alan said,

'You're safe now.'

Why shouldn't she be safe? The bell tolled nearer. Why were they watching her so intently?

Winifred said, almost apologetically, with a glance at Alan,

'I think perhaps she doesn't quite remember.'

'She will have to remember. If she refuses . . .'

'Give her time, though.' Winifred spoke so gently and softly. It was a bit like watching a play, quite an interesting one, although Winifred and Alan had got it wrong, somehow. Angela wondered if she could help the action along. She said:

'Ought I to remember you?'

This time their faces whirled round on one another. Alan said slowly,

'Yes.'

Winifred murmured: 'Be careful.'

Alan turned back to Angela. His eyes caught and held hers. But his eyes had always been direct. It was his mouth, his expression, that had changed.

'Yes,' he said, again. 'You should remember me, Angela. Alan Boyce.'

'Oh, I remember your name. But I don't know what for. How did I meet you?'

'We met on the beach at Cannes. Again in the hotel bar.'

'Cannes. Hotel bar.'

Alan's hand was gripping a piece of the bedspread. Something flashed in and out of her mind, threatening to disturb the white peace. The bell clanged, now.

'No! No! I don't want . . .'

'I sat beside you in the hotel bar. We had coffee.' Alan's hand. So close to her, as it was now. She admiring it, the sun playing over the back of it, moving as the curtain moved in the bar window, the old man shuffling past, fear because Mother and Father and Peter hadn't come. Peter? No, not Peter. Gerald. White face. Hair fallen forward. Eyes staring. But not seeing. Blood. Trickling out of the corner of his mouth. Gerald. Gerald!

'Oh, no!'

Someone was calling out and crying a long way off. Cries of outrage and appeal for the picture to dissolve. Only it wouldn't. She turned this way and that in the bed to escape it, but it wouldn't go.

Winifred had her arms round her. Her tears were falling on Winifred's cardigan sleeve. She buried her head in Winifred's arms and heard Alan's brisk quiet voice.

'Gerald's dead. Shot. He must have died instantly.'

'There were four shots.'

There was nothing, now, that she wouldn't remember, only the memories would have to take their turn. Gerald.

'Don't,' said Winifred, stroking her hair. 'Please, don't.'

'It's all right.' Alan's voice was confident. 'It's good for her to cry.'

'I know, but it's so violent . . . Ah!' Winifred started to draw away from her, and Angela clutched after the warm refuge. 'Look, dear,' said Winifred coaxingly, 'here's somebody very special to see you.'

Angela felt herself being laid back on the pillow. A hand covered hers. After a moment she opened her eyes. Alan and Winifred were standing at the window, their backs to her. Beside the bed was Daddy.

'Daddy. Oh, Daddy!'

Angela said nothing else the afternoon long. Looking at him, outlining the beloved features, holding the familiar hands. Daddy the same as ever, calm, confident, very slightly amused. Submerging her in great warm waves of reassurance. And when, eventually, she looked beyond him for Mummy, he said:

'Mummy's waiting for us at home.'

The brightest light was fading from the sky by the time Angela noticed that Alan and Winifred were no longer at the window.

'Who are they, Daddy?'

'There's rather a lot to tell you.'

'Daddy. How can Gerald be dead and I be safe?'

He took her hand between both of his. She didn't like the look of pity that came into his eyes.

'That's really the whole story,' he said.

'I want to know the whole story. I've been in the dark for so long.' Tears of self-pity welled over. Her head was aching, unfamiliarly. 'Have I been ill?'

'You've been concussed. Someone hit you on the head.'

The picture was there again, which she had taken with her into oblivion.

'I was glad they did. Oh, Daddy, I can't bear it.'

He said, when he had rocked her for a few minutes in his arms,

'Would you like to get up this evening? It's warm and lovely, and we could sit on the terrace.'

'What terrace, Daddy? Where am I?'

'Oh, darling, I forget the half of it. You're in hospital not far from Aix. The doctor said you might get up, if you wanted to.'

'I don't remember any doctor.' There had been nothing between Gerald on the flagstones, and this white room. 'If I get up, will you tell me what happened?'

'Alan will tell you.'

'Who is Alan?'

'He will tell you that, too.'

Alan and Winifred joined them a little later on the hospital terrace. Angela had walked there on Daddy's arm, leaning on it, dizzy for the first few minutes that she stood up, but knowing she was weak rather than ill. Feeling in fact agreeably small and frail for the first time since childhood. Not worrying about anything except keeping the new picture hidden until she was stronger and more used to knowing it was there.

Curious, though. Curiouser and curiouser. Had M wound up his case? Where was he? Why had death come with a coachload of tourists? What on earth had Alan Boyce to do with it all? If, during the time in Cannes, her mind had glided over the possibility of his involvement, it had been as a member of the gang. But here he was, the apparent spokesman of law and order, approved by Daddy, no longer the silly ass of the seaside. And Winifred . . .

'Feeling better?' asked Winifred tenderly, putting a rug that Angela hardly needed across her knees.

They drew their wicker chairs into a circle round her and sat silent, looking at their feet, or the view, and Angela had another stirring of alarm.

'Alan, you must talk to me!'

'All right,' said Alan, and he took a deep breath as if preparing himself for a difficult task. But he still said nothing, and the sun sank lower and drove its fingers into their eyes, inducing a sort of blindness which was not unwelcome. Below the sun, if she put her hand over the right side of her face, Angela saw a long shadowy vista of countryside. She shivered, suddenly glad of the rug. She was close enough to Daddy unobtrusively to put her hand into his.

'I think,' said Alan at last, 'that we should begin by you telling us your story, Angela.'

'But I want you to explain things to *me!* Please, Alan!'

'Of course you do, and I shall, but I shall do it better if I know what happened to you. Please, Angela! It's—very important.'

'All right. From—seeing those men?'

'From meeting Gerald.'

The sun, now, was very near the far low horizon. Daddy and Winifred both turned to her, smiling anxiously. Alan said,

'I asked the doctor . . .'

'Oh, it's all right.' Although it might be a bit difficult to recall everything over so tremendous a gap.

'Thank you.' Alan turned round and made a gesture. Angela for the first time noticed a young man sitting in the shadows. He dragged his chair forward, beside Alan. He had a notebook and a pen.

'Sergeant Evans will be taking down what you say,' Alan told Angela. 'You see, you'll be telling us a lot of things we don't know.'

'There are so many things that *I* don't know!'

'Of course. So the sooner you tell me, the sooner I shall tell you. Please.' Alan's smile wasn't really any different from what it had been in Cannes. Winifred nodded encouragingly. Daddy squeezed her hand. Angela told Alan everything she could remember. About meeting Gerald at the Playhouse and telephoning him and the Bella Ball and the dark house with the fighting outside it and the pursuit and the telephone call and the kidnap in the wood.

'Only it wasn't,' said Angela.

'Only it was,' said Winifred, and Alan said, sharply,

'No, Win!'

'I'm sorry,' said Winifred, not at all apologetically. 'But I couldn't help it. I couldn't let her say that, and leave it.'

'All right!' Alan sat forward. 'We know the rest anyway, just about.'

'What did Winifred mean?' asked Angela. She could almost have put her hands up, to ward the answer off.

'I'll tell you,' said Alan, 'but just answer me this. Have you any idea where the flat was?'

'We'd been driving about twenty minutes, I suppose, when I suddenly recognised Peachey Street—the town end, after coming through a lot of side roads. I wasn't really looking, I'd no idea where we'd started from . . .'

'That's fine,' said Alan. 'Now, what was the flat like?'

'Oh, small, thirties decor—office, lounge, two bedrooms. Top floor. Alan . . .'

'And outside? The rest of the building?'

'Cheap and nasty. Tiny lift. Sort of mottled green walls and stairs—solid pseudo-marble, you know, with a green frieze. Tomato brick outside. Small parking area. No trees. I think it was pretty towny. Oh, Alan, please.'

She had had to sit down on the bottom pseudo-marble step, and put her head between her knees. It was almost like that now.

'Won't that do?' Daddy asked Alan.

'Yes, sir, I think it will.' Alan turned to Sergeant Evans. 'All right. You've got a few things to do.'

'Yes, sir.' Sergeant Evans got to his feet.

'Use the *Préfet*'s office in Aix.'

'Yes, sir.'

Sergeant Evans left them, and Alan took Angela's other hand. The gesture, so foreign to this new Alan, frightened her further.

'What did Winifred mean? Are you a policeman?'

His face relaxed again into a smile. 'Of a kind.'

She was dreadfully dizzy. If she had been on her feet she would have fallen over.

'Tell me. Go on.'

'All right.' Why was he so reluctant to tell her things? Even now he was hesitating, looking at the sunset. 'I didn't make your acquaintance by chance, Angela,' said

Alan, 'although I learned by chance that you were in trouble.'

'In—trouble?'

'Your father is very, very rich.'

That strain again, it has a dying fall!

'I know.' The classroom, the cluster of girls, the spokeswoman, the accusation.

'So did others know. Clever men. One man in particular. And he decided to relieve your father of a goodly portion of his worldly wealth. In a very old way.'

'What way?' She wanted to know, desperately, and yet she didn't want to know at all, she wanted to tell him to stop.

'By kidnapping his daughter.'

The words dropped into the sudden dusk. The sun had disappeared over the low horizon. The long vista before them was in shades of grey, out of sight. The only colour was high up in the sky, pink against a small pack of cloud, from the vanished sun.

'But they saved me . . .'

Alan pressed her hand, pressed her into silence.

'You have been made to see everything that has happened, Angela—right from the beginning, when you met Gerald Massinger—in the wrong light. So, as I have so much to tell you, try just to sit and listen. It will all come clear.'

'All right.' She didn't want it to come clear, but until it did she would be living in a no-man's land, comfortable, phoney, the land of the amnesiac. That wouldn't do. 'Go on, Alan. I'll listen.' It was like gritting yourself against the promise of physical pain.

'That's a good Angela.' His sudden grin seemed to be for her, not just something appropriate in the circumstances. It warmed her slightly.

'A very clever man planned this operation, Angela.'

'M was clever,' agreed Angela.

'M?'

'Mr McGregor. I called him M, because—well, you know . . .'

She smiled ruefully round on them, but they weren't smiling. The men were looking grave and Winifred had her hand over her face.

'What's the matter?' Alarm squeezed her heart. 'It's all right, Daddy, it's all right. I know now, Mr McGregor wasn't a Special Branch officer. He kidnapped me.'

'Not Mr McGregor, Angela,' said Alan, 'Gerald Massinger.'

She couldn't believe what he had said, but he said it again. She pulled her hand free, shouted at him.

'No! No! You've made a mistake, you're crazy. You can't be a policeman! Not Gerald! The others, yes. But Gerald was kidnapped with me. He was my fellow-prisoner! You're mad . . .'

'No, Angela,' said Daddy. 'It was Gerald.'

'Oh, love,' said Winifred sadly. 'You'll have to believe it.'

So she sat there in silence, gradually believing it, letting the belief flow in waves of pain and weakness over her body.

She said at last, idiotically,

'He was English.'

'Oh, yes,' said Alan, 'he was English. Good family, minor public school, clever. But somehow he never fitted into any of the niches that people tried to prepare for him. He went to the States to make his fortune, and made a good living. In various illegal ways. But although he kept in the background of his enterprises (he was always a good delegator), things started to get too hot for him. He made soundings in this country, he learned about your father, and about you. He'd organised a successful kidnapping in the US a few years earlier. So he came back to the UK.'

'All right, darling?' asked Daddy.

She nodded.

'When Gerald Massinger (to stick to the name you know) arrived in this country, and looked further into his hunch, he liked it even better. So he came to your neighbourhood—to your Playhouse, Angela—because he wanted to meet you. He waited till you'd taken your "A"s and the school term was over. By that time he had recruited a team.'

'M. Mr McGregor.'

'Yes, James McGregor. A sort of provincial mafia man, but known only by his works. Worth his weight in gold to Gerald Massinger. And henchmen of McGregor's. And'—Alan paused, recrossed his legs—'his wife.'

'M's—Mr McGregor's wife.'

'No,' said Alan, staring at her, 'Mr Massinger's.'

'Oh, no!'

They kept forcing her to say that. There was no end to it. No end to her ignorance, and these waves of nausea.

'Yes, Angela. Gerald Massinger's wife.'

She whispered:

'Gerald? Married? But . . .'

'Gerald married.'

'But where was his wife?' She could still only whisper.

Carys, it must be. There had been no other woman involved except . . . *Oh no!*

'He made her play the role of his mother.'

'Oh, no, oh, Alan, Daddy . . .' She clutched Alan's arm imploringly. He took her hand again. 'She's *old* . . .'

Alan smiled, in amusement and compassion, lacing her fingers with his.

'Not so old. And an actress. And wore an ageing wig.' Those scarves! That horror of the Mistral! 'And Gerald—was not so young as he looked. The expressionless face of the amoralist doesn't seem to ship the usual stress lines.'

'Not *always* expressionless!'

But she knew what Alan meant. The few times Gerald had registered feeling in his face, she had noted and remembered it. He had, eventually, registered feeling for her. Her conviction of this was a tiny inviolable warmth under the ice of her shock. Whatever else Alan destroyed, that would be left.

But memories were surging back, and as they came they lost their innocence and grew horribly significant: Mother and Gerald coming into the bar together at noon, the morning after her encounter with Barbara, both gayer than usual, bright-eyed, *contented* (and she had battered on the connecting door and there had been no response); Mother telling her not to go to her room; M, once, snubbing Gerald, because only with Angela present would he have a chance to do it; Gerald and Mother dancing, her arms round his neck, both his round her waist, like when he was dancing with Christine Bolam; Gerald and Mother teasing each other; Gerald and Mother . . . Gerald and Mother . . . Poor Father! Angela gave a hysterical yelp. Alan waited.

'Who was—Mr Thompson?' she managed at last. She was all of a sudden trying not to *laugh*, it was extraordinary. But then, she had been made such a monumental fool of.

'Oh, one of the mafia. Wanted to get out of the UK in rather a hurry. Paid mightily for the service rendered.'

'And I thought . . .' The humiliation of it. What they had told her, and what she had swallowed. All M's rounded clichés. But at the beginning . . .

'You mean—Gerald came to Frensham just because of me, as part of his plan?'

'I'm afraid so.'

'But—he never rang me up. He was— nice, but then I didn't hear from him.'

'Exactly. So what happened?'

'I rang him. Oh!'

'Yes. He had made a study of you, Angela.' Alan spoke gently, but was making it sound impersonal, matter-of-fact. As if it was commonplace for people to make such idiots of themselves. Slipping over the implications.

'He decided that if he could—intrigue you, really capture your interest, and your concern, the operation would be so much easier to sustain.'

'And I fell for it. He was waiting . . . But I only rang him because of the Bella Ball.'

'Well, that was a break for him. He'd have rung you himself, when your contrary, youthful flame had been fanned by his seeming indifference. No state keener than youth for wanting what it apparently can't have.'

Oh, but he was being kind to her. He was trying to make her personal gullibility and immaturity sound like no more than the natural state of the young. His kindness, at least, hadn't been put on. She said, miserably:

'You hardly need to tell me any more. I fell for everything. Believed everything.' But those men, fighting! She said eagerly: 'Alan, those men though, fighting . . .'

'A tableau,' said Alan inexorably, 'devised for Angela. To justify taking you into their protection.' He pressed her hand. 'He was always thorough, Angela, he probably hoped to retire on the proceeds of this operation. He knew—that you were impressed by the spy myth, that you liked TV series and films about it. You probably told him so yourself.' She had told him a great deal, that first evening at the Playhouse. Words had tumbled out. 'At that point, he probably still had an open mind about tactics, even if his overall strategy was worked out.'

The next worse thing, after Gerald and Mother, could be summed up in a few words.

'So they were all baddies.'

Alan smiled briefly, stretched his legs. 'All baddies, yes.'

Including Gypsy. Well, that was irrelevant to Gypsy, somehow. Oh, God, what had happened to Gypsy?

'Was anybody else—killed?'

'No.'

She would let that do, to be going on with.

'It was so elaborate, Alan. Why did they take me abroad?'

'As I said, the man who played your father paid very handsomely to get abroad. And it seemed the safest thing. Would have been, but for a fluke.

Massinger had slipped out of the States unknown to the authorities and he had no sort of form in Europe—and no living relatives we gather. And—I think it was his panache, as well.'

'His panache?'

Alan, now, seemed to be looking inwards, as if he was still pondering a mystery.

'I'm going now partly on what McGregor told me. I suppose I mean that he was a sort of artist with what he did. He wanted to embellish it, to get fun out of it as well as profit. Like taking phoney passports and handing them over to the gimlet eyes of the casino boys. He wanted to flaunt his brilliance under the noses of the stupid goodies.' Alan laughed, attractively. 'I don't know,' he said, 'of course I don't *know*.'

Nor would he. Angela reflected, with a sense of satisfaction that surprised her, that Gerald had carried his mystery away with him for ever.

'So Mr McGregor has talked?'

'And how! All of them have talked. Sung to high heaven, I should say. Well, their boss is dead. You only grass on the living. People elsewhere have talked too. In the States, for instance.'

'What's happened to them all?'

'McGregor and Massinger's wife were tailed when they left the village, and picked up at the spot where the transaction was to have taken place.'

'Transaction?'

'You for the money, my darling.'

'Oh, Daddy!'

No wonder she had felt isolated. No wonder her captors had grown more and more edgy, moving up to the big kill. But she had escaped, and her captors had been caught. Those tourists, silently moving down the narrow street. Alan Boyce, watching even when she was Miss Thompson in Cannes.

'But how did anybody know to rescue me, for goodness' sake? How did anybody know where I was?'

'Well, it was a stroke of luck, really.' Alan settled back in his chair. They were all relaxing a bit now, now that they had told her the worst. 'We had a man on at Dover, the day you sailed, with a tip-off—oh, nothing to do with you, it was a red-hot foolproof tip-off about some smuggling, and he saw *you*.'

'But I wasn't . . .'

'Your photograph had been circulated, of course. Everyone was looking out for you in a general sort of a way, although there was no trail at all.'

'But I didn't look like me!'

'I know, I know. But this chappie—Bill Foster—fancies he has a talent for faces, and so he cultivates it. He says that when he saw you he took a peek at the photo of you he'd been issued with and felt there was a strong possibility. So he took another picture.'

'With his tie, I expect,' said Winifred. 'Was he wearing a bow tie?'

'I don't remember . . .'

'Shut *up*, Win! Bill was one of a team working on the other job, which was straightforward and all but wrapped up, so he signed off it, came with you on the boat and on the train, found where you were staying in Cannes, briefed me, and went home.'

'What were you doing in Cannes, though?'

'What I told you.' He grinned at her. 'On sick leave. After glandular fever. Staying with my Granny.'

'You told me Winifred's Granny.'

'Same thing. Winifred's my sister.'

'Oh, Alan!' She turned the other way. 'Winifred!'

'I'm sorry,' said Winifred. 'It was rather fun, actually.'

'We began,' said Alan, 'to enjoy the act for its own sake.'

'Like us!' said Angela excitedly. 'The way we kept the family going. Even where it wasn't really necessary. It was real.' She squeezed Daddy's hand contritely.

'That's what I was trying to say about Gerald Massinger. The hallmark of all his enterprises was thoroughness and a delight in all the trappings. Perhaps it rubbed off on us, his adversaries!'

'So, Winifred, you just became your brother's fiancée for the extra fun of it?'

Winifred looked at Alan, who said slowly:

'Well, not quite. We felt—that if we changed things, gave ourselves a reason for "acting", we'd be more vigilant, stick to it better.'

'He means me,' said Winifred, 'he's a professional.'

'But you altered your personalities as well, didn't you? Forgive me—but you seemed so daft sometimes, Alan, saying goodbye and never going, and Winifred seemed so—well, so *bossy!*'

Winifred began to giggle at that, and in a moment Alan was laughing. He laughed more and more uncontrollably, and Winifred was laughing too, swaying backwards and forwards in her chair. Angela couldn't quite join it, but she was glad to hear them.

'I'm sorry,' gasped Alan at last, wiping his eyes. 'Win said to me something about you'd better get rid of that professional manner and I said I'd always fancied a Bertie Wooster role'—'He played him once in a school play', said Winifred—'and then she said she'd better start being bossy—that was the very word, my sweet, wasn't it?—to look as if somebody was in charge of us, and it would be good because it was so far from her real self . . .'

'It *was* good.' Angela looked wonderingly at Winifred's pretty, gentle face, with its perpetually half smiling mouth. 'It was marvellous. I got to thinking you were positively dreary, I'm afraid. I felt tired just *thinking* about you in an office.'

'She paints,' said Alan, through more laughter.

'Oh, Winifred.'

'She'll tell you about it.'

'But now you want to get on. All right.' Winifred who painted, Alan's sister, was a tiny new source of warmth. Angela found that she was still talking. 'Alan, you reacted *just* like me! I felt that Caroline was a real person, someone I was taking over, someone who already had likes and dislikes and habits and opinions. I even found myself despising her for being silly, and admiring her for being sophisticated, when she wasn't *anything* unless I chose for her to be. Yet I had to be silly, and try to be sophisticated, because I had to be her.' But Angela had never taught herself the things she had learned. Some parts of it all could never be explained. 'Sorry, Alan! Go on.'

'Well, Bill gave me this unofficial assignment, and went back to the UK. I "met" you on the beach, trying out my new persona for the first time. Not knowing, then, that you had been fed a load of guff. Thinking how inhumanly brave you were—if you really were Angela Canford.'

'She was humanly brave, anyway,' said Winifred stoutly.

'But how could you be sure I was me?'

'I showed my card to the hotel authorities and impounded your passports for a couple of days with injunctions to discretion—thank heaven I got them back in time for your casino jaunt! Very interesting, those passports proved to be. Equipment at the *Sûreté* revealed them for what they were. Bill's snapshot seemed to tally with the picture of Angela Canford, when the experts got to work on it. Then—do you remember someone calling your name—calling "Angela"—in the ladies' room at the casino?'

'Yes. *Yes!* I thought it was two women in there . . . but it gave me an awful shock—I was staggering around with lipstick all over my face when Winifred came out of the loo—it was *you!* You called "Angela"!'

'Yes.'

'Gosh, you were good! I can remember you, all cool out of the loo. Hardly looking at me. But you were!'

'Well, I didn't have to look very closely. You were almost passing out.'

'And then,' said Alan, 'I reported. And Bill Foster reported. And my vigilance became official.'

'And then it was all plain sailing.'

'Well—plainer. We had a team round you.'

'A team?'

'A few people beside me.'

'And in the village?'

'Did you ever see an old man with a dog, for instance?'

'Oh, Alan!'

'And one of the school teachers.'

'No!'

'And, in the end, the tourists.'

'All of them? The whole busload?'

'It wasn't full. But yes, the whole busload!'

'A busload of detectives?'

'Well, French police. Mostly junior. But good marksmen.'

'Yes.' White and red. Gerald's face and Gerald's blood. Gerald staring, and not seeing. Suddenly she was weeping, great heavy sobs. Her chest must surely wear out, with all the weeping of the last weeks.

'Oh, *leave* her!'

Winifred was behind Angela's chair, her arms on her shoulders. Daddy gripped her hand.

Alan said, injured:

'Well, really!'

The injustice of his position helped Angela.

'I'm all right.' She took her hands away from them and blew her nose. 'Alan didn't upset me, I upset myself.'

'And will do, darling, for a long time, but less and less violently.' Daddy nodded to Alan. 'Go on.'

'We knew the transaction was about to take place,' said Alan. 'You, sir, were on your way, ostensibly to do business. We picked up McGregor and the woman. That left just Massinger, his two thugs, and the couple in the house. It should have been easy. Only one of the thugs started shooting.'

311

One of the thugs. Gypsy maybe. The smell of Gypsy came to her, griped her stomach.

'What happened to Gypsy?'

'Gypsy?'

Angela felt she was blushing. She murmured:

'Fred Bates of Petersham. I mean, Fred Bates . . .'

'Well, now,' said Alan, 'I reckon friend Fred was on the lucky side. He only lost the tip of a finger.'

'Oh, no.' The nausea swamped her again. Gypsy's hands—so articulate when he was explaining. Over her mouth. Gripping her arms. One each side of her on the bed.

'Not—lost . . .'

'Well, I don't know. I haven't learned the details of the latest events, as you'll appreciate. That was the report. Whatever the injury, it wasn't enough to keep him in hospital.'

'That means . . .'

'All remanded in custody. Back in UK, of course.'

She might find she wanted to go and see Gypsy. But it would be easier, now, to lie to Mummy and Daddy. Alan was looking at her searchingly. She said quickly:

'And—Joe Gunter?'

'Likewise. No injuries.'

Angela was suddenly very tired.

'What else?' she asked wearily.

'I don't think there need be anything else for today. Not from me, at any rate.'

'There must be lots more questions you want to ask,' said Winifred.

'I suppose so.'

But there was so much in her head already, being rejected as yet by her bewildered and reluctant mind.

Angela started to get up. She liked the Boyces. Sometime—soon—they would be friends. But just now she had had enough of them.

She was on her feet before they could help her, and she stumbled, clutching at the glass top of the table. The newspaper on it gave her fingers a grip and she steadied herself. The newspaper. Angela sat down again.

'Alan. There was never anything in the papers.'

'No. It was an unusual kidnapping, Angela, in that the kidnappers didn't tell your parents not to go to the police. They told them not to go to the media.'

'What do you mean?'

'Gerald Massinger was so confident of his organisation that he didn't fear the police. But your parents were told it would be the worse for you if they spoke to the media. And the reason isn't very hard to find: if you saw a newspaper—which they could hardly prevent you from doing—you would no longer be docile'—Angela winced and Winifred, seeing it, smiled at her—'and if the world knew, the world would be vigilant. So—that was the condition.'

'Oh, Alan, I hope it won't . . . can it go on being like that. *Please!*'

The whole nation—Europe—the *world*, would laugh at her. Oh, nobody had paid *that* price for stupidity!

'It's all right. None of our men will speak, and McGregor and Co have been warned.'

'Oh, Alan, I hope so. But if the Press get at them.'

Angela had a sudden vision of those jostling throngs with cameras who impede cars filled with unhappy, unfortunate, notorious people.

'They know that remission can be lost or won.'

The dizziness was horrible.

'I want to go back to bed now!'

She talked to Mummy before going into a long sleep, and heard from Daddy about their life since her departure. M had, indeed, telephoned them every day, but his assurances as to Angela's safety had been backed by the possibility of danger if they did not pay the money demanded, or spoke to the Press. Half a million pounds.

'And I worried so much about you, Daddy—all the time now I look back, although I tried to pretend I wasn't. Thinking of the house being watched by those terrible men. Oh, Daddy, I've not taken it in yet, they didn't exist . . . Or that bossy spinsterish Winifred, or Alan as he seemed. I knew the Thompson family wasn't real, but nothing else was, either.'

'Your good angel was real enough. And the house *was* watched. By good men and bad!'

She asked, sleepily:

'When are we going home?'

'Not for a few days. You're not your tough old self quite yet. Here, take your pill and go to sleep.'

There were regular pills. No doubt helping her to absorb the retrospective horrors, even of Gerald's death, and get better.

Because she was getting better. The next day she got dressed and walked in the hospital grounds. The day after, she and Daddy visited Daudet's *moulin* at Fontvieille in a hired car and she did half the driving. The day after they had tea in a restaurant on Les Baux, looking down the Val d'Enfer where Raymond de Turenne, flail of Provence, had forced his prisoners to leap for his amusement.

'Oh, Daddy,' said Angela, her mouth full of gâteau, 'these are *quiet* days compared to those.'

They walked round Arles, and Salon with its mossy fountain. They poked into Greek ruins, travelled long straight roads bordered by plane trees, tried to guess places where Van Gogh had stood.

It was hard to understand how you could be struggling against obscene memories, and yet be intensely happy.

On the last day, Alan and Winifred came from Le Cannet to see her. She walked with them in the gardens and they all talked fascinatingly about their impromptu acting careers, about the strange excitement, which they had each one been aware of, of their roles, and the more solid pleasure of being together as themselves. Winifred told Angela about the paintings she was working on.

'I wish I could see them.'

'I wish you could, but your father is taking you home tomorrow, and you want to go.'

'Yes, of course I do, but I'd like . . . Are you staying much longer, Winifred?'

'I'm going to squeeze another few weeks. We'll meet in England.'

'I hope so, Winifred, I really do. Where do you live?'

'London.'

'Both of you?' asked Angela a bit hesitantly, and Alan said, 'Both of us.'

Winifred leaned against a tree and wrote one address and one telephone number on a piece of paper torn out of her diary.

'Thanks,' said Angela, glancing involuntarily at Alan.

'We live together,' said Winifred, 'up to now.'

'We know your address already,' said Alan, 'and your telephone number.'

They were both so nice and kind, standing there smiling at her, Angela felt tears coming.

'I can never, never thank you . . .'

'Please don't try!' said Winifred.

'So I was being looked after by Special Branch, after all.'

'I'm in the Civil Service,' said Alan severely.

'Oh, I know.' They had to say that.

'That's strictly true,' said Winifred. 'It's thanks to you I've at last learned which department!'

'Thanks to me?'

'Yes. You see, they needed my help in the end so they had to tell me. Now we must both keep his secret, forget all about it.'

'Of course we will.' Of course she would keep his secret. But she wouldn't forget.

'You never showed me the *Fondation Maeght*. Do you really dislike it so much, Winifred?'

Winifred hesitated. 'I don't know, really. I was sort of trying dislike out to see if it fitted. I still don't know.'

'She disliked it because I didn't,' said Alan. 'She enjoyed herself over that.'

'Playing the game for its own sake,' said Angela. 'But you hesitated, Winifred, when you said you hadn't any brothers!'

'When you're forced into a direct lie, you feel you aren't playing the game very well.'

'Oh, I know what you mean!'

She was certain this was not the only subtlety which she would agree with Winifred and Alan. Their friendship could add another dimension to her life.

They stood on the lawn below the terrace, in the last patch of sunshine.

'By the way,' said Alan, 'my sick leave's over. I'll be on the plane with you tomorrow.'

'Oh, Alan!'

'And one other small revelation. The last one, my dear. Boyce is my middle name. Holland our mother's maiden name. Cartwright on my passport. And Winifred's.'

'Passport! Alan, I haven't got mine!'

'Your father brought it.'

Caroline's brother had reassured her about her passport in the casino, in almost the same words. It would be a long time before those memories let her alone. And one of them never would.

'Can I have that phoney passport back eventually, Alan? Unless it has to go into a black museum, or something.'

'No, it doesn't, and I'll get it back for you.' He put his fist against her cheek, friendly and unromantic. 'Are you all right now?'

'Yes, I think so.'

Winifred had left them, strolled over to examine a blossom tree against a hedge.

'I'm sorry—about Massinger.'

'Yes. That was the worst. That's the only thing I've really got to recover from, actually. I saw him. Blood coming out of his mouth. Dead and staring.' It was good to say it aloud, it forced her to believe and accept. 'I'd dreamed about it. Not just once. It was almost as if I knew it would happen. Oh, Alan.' She put her head against his shoulder, waited a moment for the image to disappear. It was going to be like a mental seizure, every now and then, or a knife in her heart. Winifred had got into conversation with a nurse.

'It will pass away. I'm sorry, though—he made you so fond of him.'

She looked at him in surprise, realising something.

'Oh, Alan, he didn't make me in love with him—not in the least!'

'Didn't he?' It was Alan's turn to be surprised.

'Oh, at the start I was bowled over, I suppose. And exactly as you said, when he didn't come up to scratch I got all the keener. But when I got to know him . . . it's funny, really, I got to like him, I thought, more and more, but that— other—didn't develop.' *I know a lady would have walked barefoot to Palestine for a touch of his nether lip.* 'Oh, Alan, life is so *complicated!*'

'I'm afraid it is. But I'm glad you didn't think you were in love with him.' He smiled at her. 'Shows the right instinct.'

'Yes.' She would leave it at that. She couldn't explain to Alan, because she couldn't properly explain to herself, that what she had felt for Gerald had been as important as being in love. And what Gerald had felt for her—he hadn't in the end, she was sure, wanted to deceive her, to use her, and so the memory of what he had done wasn't horrible.

In fact Gerald Massinger had come to love her. But this she would tell to no one, not even Mummy or Daddy. She didn't want to tell anyone, but even if she did, they wouldn't believe her. They would think she was off her head with conceit.

Well, she was more conceited than she had been. She didn't think that anything was automatically out of her reach.

Gerald had done that for her.

Alan was looking at the sunset, its gold suffused his face. Alan Boyce Cartwright.

She wouldn't have to change the initials on her silver dressing-table set . . .

But she wouldn't want to get married for ages and ages, although she would want to love.

Gypsy had done that for her.

'What's up?' asked Alan.

'Alan,' she said casually, recovering quickly from the shock of another memory, 'I suppose the police took everything away from the house in the village?'

'Yes?'

'It was just . . . my diary was in my room. With some books I was reading. Will they let me have them back? I'd like to have them back.'

Thank goodness she had burned those pages. But she still thought she had not been entirely discreet. Her mind sought after the extant pages of her diary, while she looked hard at Alan, and he looked hard at her. Had he read it? She didn't think he would ever let her know.

'Oh, yes,' he said, at last. 'I'll see to it that you get them back.'

'Thanks.'

Darting a kiss at his cheek, eluding his hand, running away from him up the flight of steps to the terrace, two at a time, Angela pushed through the glass doors without a backward glance.

Caroline had done that for her.